SHOTS

Judy Kay

PublishAmerica
Baltimore

First printing

All characters in this book are fictitious, and any resemblance to real persons, living or dead, is coincidental.

PublishAmerica has allowed this work to remain exactly as the author intended, verbatim, without editorial input.

ISBN: 1-60672-371-5
PUBLISHED BY PUBLISHAMERICA, LLLP
www.publishamerica.com
Baltimore

Printed in the United States of America

Also by Judy Kay
Dead Art

To Sharon and Peaches,
Two of the prettiest
blonds in the dog Park!.

Judy Kay

This book is dedicated to
Nancy Perry and Katie Casey
Thanks for all your encouragement!

Chapter One

Saturday, April 7, 2:32 p.m.

"Do you Abigail take thee…" Shots rang out and Brandon fell to the ground.

"Get down, get down. Everybody get down." The best man shouted as he grabbed Abby and dragged her down trying to shield her with his body while at the same time trying to spot the shooter. She was screaming and struggling beneath him as he held her down protecting her as best he could. It took all his strength to hold her and keep her from squirming out from under him to get to Brandon. Several more shots rang out and Jack saw the minister crumple to the ground and a lady in the first row toppled forward onto the grass, her horrified husband looking on in disbelief. Jack chanced a glance around and thought he saw a muzzle flash from the bell tower window and then a shadow cross quickly behind the window.

"Jack, Let me up. I have to see about Brandon."

"Not now Abby, stay down until its safe."

Brandon's mom and dad crawled over to where Jack was holding Abby and they huddled there trying to take in the fact that someone was shooting at them. Everyone was screaming and knocking over chairs in their haste to get to a safe place. Guests were running into the chapel. Jerry made his way over to Kristen, who was the maid of honor and also Jerry's current girl friend. "Come on Kristen, you need to get inside." Jerry told her.

With tears running down her face, she looked at him. "My God, what's happening? Who is shooting?" She asked.

"I don't know, but you've got to get inside." He put his arm around her and caught her mother with his other arm. "Come on, Mrs. Schwartz, I need to get you and Kristen inside. There isn't anything you can do out here. Come inside where you will be safe." Jerry finally got them moving toward the chapel, one arm around each of them, shielding them with his body as best he could, looking all around trying to spot the shooter.

Mothers and fathers were herding their children between them, glancing in all directions, not knowing where the shots had come from or which way to run. Jack put a hand on Abby's back. "Listen to me. I'm going to try to get Brandon. You stay right here, stay down and don't move. Do you understand me?" Abby nodded at Jack as he made his way over closer to Brandon. He tried to drag Brandon over to them by his pant leg but he was too heavy. Brandon's dad crawled up to where Jack was and he and Jack dashed out and grabbed Brandon and pulled him over behind some overturned chairs which provided them a little shelter if someone was still shooting. Jack put two fingers on the pulse point in Brandon's neck but couldn't detect a pulse. There was a small hole in the back of Brandon's tuxedo jacket. Jack rolled Brandon over and saw the large exit wound where the bullet had gone all the way through Brandon. Pete ran up and ducked down beside them. "What the hell is happening, oh, my God, they shot Brandon." He shouted. Like Jack, he immediately checked for a pulse. He looked at Jack with dismay when he saw the wound in Brandon's chest. He knew that there wasn't any hope.

Jack looked over the crowd and saw the minister was down in a pool of blood directly in front of them and the woman who had been sitting in the front row was now laying face down on the lawn with a large blood stain in the middle of her back. He saw several of the guests with blood on their clothes but he couldn't tell if they were injured or if the blood was from someone else. He looked toward where his mom and dad had been sitting and saw them crouching on the ground. His mother looked terrified and his dad looked up and nodded to Jack that they were ok. Jack motioned for them to get inside the chapel. He watched as his dad put his arm around his mother and they started toward the chapel. His mother looked back at Jack to make sure he was ok. Jack scanned the area again trying to determine if the shooting was over and if he could see anyone who looked out of place at the wedding.

Abby was leaning over Brandon, the bright crimson blood soaking into the white satin and lace of her beautiful wedding dress, her blood stained hand covering the ugly wound in his chest trying unsuccessfully to stop the flow of blood. He could see where she had wiped her bloody hands on the dress. She looked at Jack with tear filled eyes and he knew Abby realized that Brandon was gone. Abby's mother and dad had crawled over to Abby and Abby's mother had her arms around Abby. Brandon's mother was kneeling on the ground beside her son. In seconds, the shots stopped and pandemonium reigned. "Call 911." Jack shouted as he pulled out his own cell phone and dialed the police station as several other people grabbed their cell phones and started calling. "This is Detective Oakley. We have shots fired at the rear of the Episcopal Church on Piney Point at Memorial. Civilians down. Need assistance immediately." He shouted into the phone. Pete grabbed his mom and dad and was hurrying them into the chapel away from Abby and Brandon.

Jack lifted Abby to her feet and said "Come on Abby, we've got to get you inside where it's safe."

"I can't leave Brandon. He's hurt."

"You have to leave him. I've got to get you inside. You can't do any more for him. Come on Carol and Ted. You need to get inside, I'll bring Abby to you." He took her elbow and forced her to move toward the chapel all the while scanning the building and surroundings to see if he could spot the shooter. She was straining against him and looking back at Brandon, lying bloody and still on the ground. Jack shouted at his mom and dad to hurry and get inside.

Everyone was crowding the doors at once trying to force their way inside. Once inside, people were crying and screaming and trying to locate loved ones. It was stifling hot with that many bodies packed into the chapel and narthex and the noise level was incredible. Everyone was shouting, trying to be heard over the chaos. Guests were milling around, terrified to go outside and terrified to stay where they were. Jack found Abby's parents standing close to the door leading to the narthex watching for them to come in. He handed Abby off to her father and started pushing his way through the crowd. He tried to make his way to the bell tower door but the swarming mass of humanity prevented him from reaching it. Once again, he looked over the guests trying to see if he could spot anyone who looked out of place or who didn't belong at the wedding. He recognized almost everyone as he had known most of them for years. Everyone he saw was dressed for the wedding. Of course, if a shooter were smart, he would dress as a guest so as not to stand out in the crowd. Jack made his way through the crush of humanity until he was able to get back outside. He yelled once again for everyone to try to get inside the chapel. Brandon's mom and dad were leaning over Brandon's lifeless body crying. Jack looked around as he went toward them. He eased Brandon's mom into a standing position and held out his hand to help Brandon's dad up. He turned them toward the chapel and gave them a gentle nudge. "You need to go inside now. You can't do any more for Brandon. Please, go inside, it's not safe out here." He saw the minister was still down and there were several people kneeling around him, his wife was holding his blood soaked body in her lap. The woman who had been sitting in the front row hadn't moved and her husband was weeping over her and trying to revive her. Several people were standing over them. From the amount of blood that Jack could see on the front of her pale pink dress, he knew that she was probably already dead. She had been shot through the back and he could see the large exit wound where her husband had turned her over face up on the grass.

Crouching down, Jack made his way over to where the minister lay, glancing frequently around the perimeter to see if he could spot anything or anyone out of the ordinary. He checked for a pulse on the minister and found none. The group around the minister looked at Jack but didn't move, their eyes wide with fright. The minister's wife didn't want to let go of her husband. Jack gently eased her into a standing position and handed her off to a man standing beside them. "Take her inside where it's safe. All of you need to get inside." He gave them a gentle nudge toward the chapel.

Next he moved to woman who was down. Jack pulled out his badge and held it up. "I need everyone to get inside right now." The guests were in a state of shock and not comprehending what he was saying. Jack could hear sirens coming from several different directions screaming toward the church. He moved over to the woman in the front row and saw that she still wasn't moving. There was blood on her husband's jacket but he couldn't tell if it was from his wife or if he was injured. "Are you injured?" He asked the man.

"No, but my wife is hurt." The man had turned his wife over and was still trying to revive her.

Jack took hold of the man and brought him to a standing position. "I'm sorry, she's gone. Please go inside. You can't help her anymore." He then guided him toward the chapel and away from his wife's bloody body. The man was in shock and barely functioning. He pushed the man inside the church telling him to stay there and then Jack ran around to the front of the chapel just as the first squad cars were arriving.

As police officers started piling out of the squad cars, Jack stepped forward showing his detective badge and identification. "I think the shots came from the bell tower. I don't know if the shooter is still up there or if he got away before people came inside. I didn't see anyone shooting nor anyone running away. I counted 8 shots in all, sounded like a rifle. There are three civilians dead out back and I don't know how many more are wounded. The shots only lasted a minute or two and then we didn't hear any more shots." He looked around to see if he could see Jerry, but there were too many people. As he glanced around he saw police were cordoning off the street at both ends of the block.

He had barely finished speaking when the officers fanned out around the building with several of the officers going inside and the others splitting up and circling around toward the back of the church. Jack saw four ambulances pull up in front of the church. "Around back. They need you around back." Jack shouted as he went up the stairs of the church and made his way back inside. He pushed and shoved his way through the loud crowd back to where Abby was huddled with her parents. Her father had one arm around his sobbing daughter and the other arm around his distraught wife. Ted looked up at Jack with despair written all over his face.

"Thank you for getting Abby down when the shooting started. I froze and couldn't move until you started shouting. Is Brandon…?" Jack could tell from Ted's expression, that he knew Brandon was gone. Jack looked around but couldn't see Brandon's family.

Sadly, Jack shook his head. "He didn't make it. The minister and another woman were hit also. I've got to go now and help the officers outside. Take care of Abby, don't let her come back outside." He gave all of them a quick hug just as Jerry brought Kristen and Mrs. Schwartz over to Abby and her parents.

"Stay here with Abby so I know where to find you." Jerry said, planting a quick kiss on her trembling lips. "I'm needed outside, I'll be back as soon as I can."

Jack and Jerry walked away from them and were finally able to make their way through the mass of humanity and over to the stairs leading to the bell tower. Two of the officers were coming down the stairs. Jack and Jerry stepped aside so the officers could exit the stairwell. "Did you see anything up there?"

"Window's wide open. Could have been where the shots were fired from. We didn't find any casings. Bobby and another officer are still up there until the crime team can come in and check for prints. If that was where the shots came from, looks like the guy was careful so we probably won't find his prints."

Jack and Jerry ran up the stairs and stepped inside the dusty bell tower being careful not to touch any surfaces. The huge bell took up a lot of space in the center of the tower. Sunlight filtered through the narrow open arches showing dust mites dancing in the bands of light across the old wooden floor. They could see footprints in the dust but they knew there had been at least four officers up here so they couldn't tell if any of the footprints belonged to the shooter or just the officers. Bobby stepped aside and Jack walked to the third arch from the left. He had a perfect view of the courtyard, looking out, he was careful not to touch the ledge, just in case there were prints to be lifted. In the courtyard below, several officers were conducting interviews and one officer sat with the minister's wife trying to get her statement. He could see two or three people examining wounds on themselves and he heard more ambulances coming down San Felipe and Memorial. Shortly thereafter, Jack saw the EMTs come around the side of the chapel and go over to Brandon and then on to the other two bodies. Even this high up he could hear the crackling of their walkie talkies. A few minutes later, another EMT came around the side of the chapel and carefully covered the bodies with sheets to get them out of view. Jack was glad they covered the bodies so he wouldn't have to see Brandon laying there with the life drained out of him. Jack saw there were three other people injured besides the three that were killed. *What kind of crazy sick bastard would shoot up a wedding*, Jack thought to himself.

He doubted that the interviews of the wedding guests would be worth much. Like him, everybody had their backs to the church and had been focused on the happy, young couple exchanging their wedding vows in the beautiful gazebo outside the church. Hell, he and Jerry were detectives and they hadn't even noticed much except for what Jack thought was a muzzle flash and his automatic reaction counting the shots as he tried to protect Abby. After the shooting started, there was such pandemonium with people rushing around and shouting that they wouldn't have noticed anything behind them. It would have been easy for someone to slip away during all the commotion after the shooting. Jack thought it probably would be more helpful to interview the people passing by the church right after the shooting than from the wedding guests. He wondered if they had seen anyone leaving the church? Had the neighbors seen anyone strange in the neighborhood? If it was a rifle, how did the shooter conceal it as he walked away or did he hide it somewhere on the premises to be picked up later. There were a lot of hiding places in a big church like this. Jack knew the officers would go over the grounds and the buildings thoroughly. It was a warm and sunny April day, so chances are the shooter wasn't wearing a long coat that could conceal a rifle. *Maybe the shooter could have hidden the rifle in some kind of package or broken the rifle down so it was more portable.* There were far more questions than there were answers. His thoughts tumbled over themselves trying to make sense of this tragedy that made no sense at all. *My God*, he thought, *I can't believe they shot Brandon.*

Chapter Two

It was several hours later when the police finally started letting the weary and bedraggled guests leave the chapel. The officers had interviewed all of the guests but didn't get any answers. Men and women alike were disheveled from the heat. The air conditioning in the church wasn't set low enough to combat all the warm bodies that were crowded in the church. No one expected everyone to be inside on this beautiful day. The wedding guests were supposed to be outside, not huddled inside in fear. Many of the men had taken their jackets off and loosened their ties. Everyone was hot, tried and frightened. Most of the women had mascara running down their faces and their makeup was streaked from their tears. Children were tired, cranky and hungry and clinging to their parents in fright. Jack could hear loud snatches of conversation all around him, no one could understand why someone would shoot up a wedding. Jack had experienced that kind of nervous loud talk in crisis situations before. He knew the guests would be on the phone calling everyone they knew and telling them to watch the six o'clock news to hear about the shooting and to tell them how close each of them had been to getting killed. The story would grow more and more spectacular with every telling. He knew this was a day none of them would ever forget. It was a day he wished to hell he could forget, but he knew he never would. He wanted to go to Abby, but that would have to wait.

Jack had known Abby and Brandon since the second grade. His mom and dad had moved here from Chicago when his dad got a big promotion and was transferred to the Houston office of Merrill Lynch. Their big old house on the pretty tree lined street had sold quickly and the move was made before Jack even had a chance to get used to the idea of moving. It seemed like one minute his dad was telling him they would be moving and the next minute he was telling all his buddies goodbye and waving to them from the back seat of their Buick as his dad drove away. It was a great opportunity for his dad, but Jack hated to leave his friends. Jack was dreading going to the strange new school in Houston where he didn't know anyone. On the first day of school, the principal brought Jack into the classroom and introduced him. The teacher smiled at him and lead him to a seat behind a cute little dark haired girl in a yellow sun dress, who smiled at him as he walked by. She wore her long dark hair in two ponytails tied with yellow ribbons that matched her dress. He even remembered her little patent leather shoes that buckled across her instep and the cute little white socks trimmed in yellow to match her dress. When it came time for lunch, everybody began filing out of the classroom and left Jack sitting there. The little dark haired girl looked back at him sitting there all alone. She came back into the classroom and offered to show him the way to the cafeteria. They filled their trays, picked up their cartons of chocolate milk and Abby led the way over to a table occupied by three little boys. He was surprised when she sat down at the table with the boys. She took a seat beside the red haired boy with a face full of freckles. "This is Brandon. That one over there is Pete, he's my brother and that other mug is Jerry. He doesn't like anyone." With that, Jerry stuck his tongue out at her and Abby responded by crossing her eyes at him. Jack laughed and Abby winked and grinned at him. "You can sit here with us." From that day forward, the five of them were inseparable.

The five kids all lived in the same neighborhood within blocks of each other, so it was natural that they would walk to and from school together and hang out after school. Most afternoons after school would find all of them at one house hanging out until dinner time. The parents didn't worry about them because they knew where one was, in all probability the other four would be also. The kids were fiercely protective of one another and the other kids soon learned to mess with one of them was to mess with all of them. As they got a little older, they rode their bikes to school and locked them all together with one long chain and a padlock. Abby wouldn't hear of having a pink "girly" bike. She had to have a black boy's bike just like the guys had though it was hard for her little short legs to reach the pedals over the center bar. Until she got a little taller, she always rode her bike standing up pedaling with the tips of her toes going hell bent for Texas after the boys. She was a little tomboy and she was seldom without a skinned knee or elbow. Once a baseball had caught her off guard and she ended up with a black eye. Jack had halfway loved Abby ever since the first time he saw her, but her pretty brown eyes were always on Brandon. Brandon and Pete were a year older than the rest of them and Brandon was the first of them to get his driver's license and then the first one to get a car. When they were going somewhere, he would pick up Abby and Pete first, Abby would ride in the middle between her brother and Brandon. Next, Brandon would pick up Jerry and Jack, who would ride in the back. At their senior prom, they all had dates, of course Abby went with Brandon. Their parents got together and rented a long white limousine to take them to the prom, then to a restaurant and home afterwards. They really thought they were something that night riding in the limousine. Jack couldn't remember what his date wore or even who she was, but he remembered that Abby had worn a beautiful white strapless gown with white orchids in her dark hair. Brandon had bought her an orchid wrist corsage to match the flowers in her hair and she looked like a fairy princess that night.

The five of them had gone through grade school, high school and then to the University of Texas together, Pete and Brandon a year ahead of the other three. The boys had all played baseball for UT and Abby never missed a game. The most famous alumnus was Roger Clemens who played baseball at UT and then went on to pitch for the New York Yankees. They were thrilled to meet Roger at one of the homecoming weekends and had him autograph a baseball for each of them. He pitched for one season with the Houston Astros and then went back to the Yankees. They never missed an Astros game when Roger was pitching either for the Astros or when he was in town pitching against the Astros. The four boys all had dreams of playing in the majors, but none of them were quite good enough. They never lost their love of the game. After graduation, Jerry and he had gone to the police academy together and both made detective this year, Pete became a Houston Firefighter and Brandon landed a job as a geologist with one of the big oil companies. Abby had her teaching degree and was to start teaching at Kincaid, a private elementary school, in August. They had their lives all planned out. Brandon and Abby had planned a week long honeymoon in St. Barts and then to live happily every after. The five of them assumed they would all marry, buy houses in the same neighborhood, have kids, the kids would be friends and life would be good in their fairy tale dreams.

No one was the least bit surprised when Brandon proposed to Abby that night after the UT Oklahoma State football game.

Brandon had bought the two carat solitaire engagement ring and showed it to Pete, Jerry and Jack. He had it all planned out and swore the guys to secrecy. Jack, Jerry and Pete all had dates and the four couples had gone out to a fancy steakhouse after the game where Brandon had made reservations. Three strolling violinists came to the table and began playing. Jack, Jerry and Pete tried without success to keep a straight face. The maître d' came over with two dozen red roses followed by a waiter with two bottles of champagne and glasses. Abby looked around the table and frowned at the way the guys were grinning and looking down at the table trying their best not to give the secret away. None of them would look her in the eye. The maître d' handed Abby the roses then opened the bottles of champagne and set them in the ice buckets. He handed each of them a champagne flute and stood back smiling at them. Abby began looking around the table and everyone was grinning like fools. Brandon got down on one knee and pulled out the ring. Abby's brown eyes opened wide and then the tears started to fall. She began laughing, jumping up and kissing Brandon and yelling, "Yes, Yes, Yes, I'll marry you. I've been waiting for this my entire life!" The people in the restaurant were all smiling at the happy couple. Jack had been the first to propose a toast and to congratulate them, even though he was a little envious of their great love. He was a handsome man and had dated lots of women but he had never found anyone to make that kind of commitment. When the women he dated started getting serious, he always managed to find some fault with them. Abby and her mom had spent the entire spring perfecting the plans for this big outdoor wedding. The shooting was not in their plans, how could anyone even conceive of a disaster like this.

Chapter Three

Jack hung around while the other officers were questioning guests and people from the neighborhood. No one saw anything before the shots rang out. None of the neighbors saw anyone strange in the neighborhood, no one saw anyone dressed inappropriately, and no one saw anyone carrying a long package that could conceal a rifle. One lady who lived three houses from the church had seen an old red pick up truck drive down her street right after the shooting but hadn't paid much attention to it. The only reason she noticed it at all was because it was rather noisy. She thought the shots was the truck backfiring. At the time, she thought it probably belonged to someone's yard man because it was old and battered up. She hadn't paid any attention to the driver or noticed if there was more than one person in the truck. In other words, after all the interviews, it was a complete dead end. They probably wouldn't learn anything else until they turned up the bullets. If they could find the bullets, they could at least tell if there was more than one shooter or if all the shots came from the same gun. Jack didn't think one shooter would have had time to use more than one gun as quickly as the shots were over.

Jack looked around the church yard and caught sight of the wedding photographer busy snapping photos, not for a photo album that could be shown to friends and relatives in memory of a happy day, but perhaps in gruesome curiosity. It wasn't every day a wedding photographer got to take pictures of gunshot victims. Jack saw him take pictures of the sheet draped bodies and close ups of the people still left in the courtyard. The photographer would never forget this day either. Jack remembered he had been taking photos of the guests before the wedding had started. *Perhaps they could spot something in those photos,* Jack thought. He was sure the chief would be interested in studying those photographs also. Jack made his way over to the photographer, "We will need copies of all the photos you took today. It's possible you caught something on film that will help us find the shooter, someone or something we might have missed."

"Sure, as soon as I'm finished here, I'll get back to my studio and get to work on them. I should have them developed by tomorrow and I will drop them by the police station."

"Thanks man. Here's my card, if you need to call me."

As Jack walked back through the chapel, he passed by the white wicker baskets with the big pink bows holding birdseed packets. Each of the magenta netting bundles of birdseed was tied with pink ribbons ready to be handed to the wedding guests. Abby and her mother knew the birds would clean up the seeds, whereas church personnel would have to sweep up rice if they used that. Another detail planned by Abby and her mom to add to the perfect wedding. As Jack walked to his car, he looked at the mud and Brandon's blood on his tuxedo and the grief hit him like a brick wall. When the shooting started, he had switched into his "cop" mode and turned his emotions off. The sight of his friend's blood on his clothes turned those emotions back on. He looked over at Brandon's black Lincoln Navigator all gaily decorated for the wedding, "Just Married" printed in white shoe polish on the back window, long ropes of beer cans tied to the bumper and streamers of crepe paper tied everywhere. He, Pete and Jerry had been horsing around and laughing and joking as they decorated the car just a few short hours ago. They had been saving their beer cans for weeks to decorate the car. With a heavy heart, he walked over and unhooked the ropes of beer cans and crepe paper streamers they had tied to the bumper earlier and carried them over to a trash can where he dropped them. He went back inside and got some wet paper towels and wiped off the "Just Married" and the other things written on the windows. Later on, he would get with Jerry and take the car to a car wash before they took it back to Brandon's house, he didn't want Brandon's parents to have to look at the gaily decorated car after what had happened. He threw his bloody coat across the seat of his SUV and started the car. He took one last look at the activity around the church and sadly shook his head as he drove out of the church parking lot with tears streaming down his face.

Jack didn't have any idea what he could say to Abby or to Brandon's folks to help them through this. He was nearly numb with grief himself. Abby's mom and dad, Carol and Ted, were like second parents to him and he didn't know what to say to them either, but he turned on Memorial to go to their house. He couldn't face Brandon's parents just yet. As he pulled up, he saw his parents' car, along with Pete and Jerry's cars. A lot of people had come here to console Abby and her family. Brandon's house was probably packed with friends offering what comfort they could to his family. Jack took a deep breath and walked in the house dreading having to face Abby. At first glance, it seemed like there were too many people in the large living room, but everyone there was either a very close friend or family. The bedraggled guests still had on their wedding attire, Abby's blood stained dress was a grim reminder of what they had been through. He looked across the room and caught Abby's eye. Abby saw Jack the minute he walked in the door and she broke free of her mother's arms and ran to him.

"Jack, what am I going to do," she cried. "I can't go on without Brandon. What will I do without him?" He held her close to him as his tears fell on her silky hair. Pete and Jerry made their way over to them and the four of them huddled together, hugging each other, their grief simply overwhelming them. The room got quiet as everyone tried not to look at the grieving foursome. Jack's parents and Abby's parents were sitting together talking quietly in the corner. They looked at Abby and the three men and knew their hearts were breaking. The five kids had always been so close, this would be terrible for all of them.

Jack looked over Abby's head at Pete and Jerry. "Did either of you see anything?" Jack asked quietly.

"Let's go in the library where it's more private. Abby, why don't you go upstairs and get out of that dress?" Pete said.

"No, I have to be with the three of you."

Pete caught his mother's eye and motioned for her to come over. "Mom, why don't you take Abby upstairs and help her change out of that dress? Abby, go with mom. You can join us after you've changed. It's too hard looking at you in that dress. I just can't do it." Abby looked down at her blood soaked gown as if she had forgotten what she had on. Pete knew if she wouldn't change the dress for herself, she would do it for him. Pete was only one year older than Abby, the same age as Brandon and had always been her protector. She idolized her big brother.

Carol put her arm around Abby "Come on upstairs, Honey. I'll help you get changed. Pete's right, it's too hard to see you in that dress." Carol turned Abby and gently guided her upstairs while Pete, Jerry and Jack headed into the library. Ted caught Jack's eye and came over to join them. They closed the door behind them and walked over to the bar. For a moment, the men looked at each other, grief etched on their faces not knowing what to say. "I'm going to have a brandy, does anyone else want one?" Pete asked. The men all nodded and Pete put five brandy snifters on the bar and poured a hefty drink into each glass. The men knew that Abby would be back in a few minutes.

"The first thing I saw when I heard the shots was Brandon collapsing after the first shot. I think it was the first shot. I looked around to make sure Kristen was ok. I counted eight shots, is that what you heard, Jack?" Jerry asked.

"Yes, that's what I thought I heard. I saw Brandon fall and I looked around and saw the minister and that woman on the first row go down. Then I grabbed Abby and forced her to the ground. Did you see where the shots came from?"

"I think they came from the south side of the bell tower. I caught a glimpse of a muzzle flash. That makes sense since both Brandon and Mrs. Hall were both shot in the back and the minister was shot in the chest. It must have been a high powered rifle because the shots were through and through. Maybe a sniper's rifle." Jerry stated.

"What's going to happen now?" Ted asked.

"Well the police will go over the chapel and the grounds looking for anything to connect to the shooter. They hadn't found any casings when I left so that indicates that the shooter or shooters probably picked up their casings. They will check for fingerprints in the bell tower, but it's my guess that they won't find the shooter's prints if he was smart enough to pick up his shell casings. When I went up to the bell tower, I had a perfect view of the courtyard so I bet that's where all the shots came from. Sounds like a professional to me. They will probably bring in a metal detector to go over the grounds to try to find the bullets if they can to determine if the shots all came from one gun or more. Whoever the shooter or shooters were, they were careful. I don't understand why anyone would want to shoot Brandon or the minister or Mrs. Hall. And why do it at the wedding? It makes me wonder if Brandon was the target or was it the minister or Mrs. Hall. Might turn out it was just random and he or they didn't care who they shot. Thank God, Abby wasn't hit."

They turned as one when the door to the library opened and a pale and trembling Abby stepped inside and quietly closed the door behind her. She had changed out of her wedding dress into jeans and a black tee shirt. Her feet were bare and her face scrubbed clean. Her face was so pale it was nearly translucent. Her eyes were red from weeping and she was hanging on to her composure by a thread. Pete picked up the remaining glass of brandy and handed it to her.

"Here Abby, drink this. Come here and sit down." Pete guided her gently to a chair and she sank down into it, cradling the brandy snifter in her shaking hands. Pete sat on the arm of the chair with his arm around her. She sipped the brandy looking over the rim of the glass at all of them with her sad, tear-filled eyes.

Jack drank the brandy, and sat the glass on the bar. "I'm going to run by home and change clothes and then I am going to the station. Jerry, do you want to come with me?"

"I'll meet you at the station. I want to change out of this monkey suit before I go. Pete, take care of Abby. We will call you later if we find out any more about the shooting." They each pressed a kiss on Abby's forehead and shook Ted's hand as they went out the door.

Jack found his mom and dad with Carol. He took his mom aside and told her he was going to the station for a while and that he would call her later. She hugged him, thinking to herself, *I know it's selfish, but I'm glad it wasn't Jack who was shot.* "How's Abby doing?"

"Just barely holding on."

"How are you doing?"

"About the same." Jack said heading for the door.

Her eyes told him she understood how desolate he was feeling. The five of them were like the five musketeers as they used to laugh and call themselves. Some day they would learn to laugh again, but the loss would be with them for the rest of their lives. She hugged Jack fiercely before he walked out the door. She knew they would never forget Brandon. After Jack and Jerry had left, Jack's mother took Carol aside. "Carol, what do you want to do about the reception? Shall I call the club and let them know what happened so they don't expect us and arrange to have the food delivered to a charity, maybe the Star of Hope? It's a shame to let it go to waste."

"Oh, I hadn't even thought about the reception. Someone needs to call the club. They might have heard it on the news, but go ahead and call them. That's a good idea about Star of Hope. Thanks for doing that, God, I feel so sorry for Brandon's parents and for the kids. I don't know how Abby is going to handle all of this. I suppose we should go over there for a while, but Lord knows I am dreading it. It is bad enough here with Abby."

"Let me call the club and then Sam and I will go with you to Brandon's house." Karen said.

Abby's mom stepped over to the library door and opened it slowly. Abby was still sitting in the chair and Pete had his arm around her. Ted was standing at the bar looking out the window and lost in thought. Carol stepped inside and gently closed the door behind her. Stepping over to the chair where Abby sat, she asked "Abby, do you and Pete want to come with us to Susan and Bob's? I'm sure they would understand if you are not up to it."

"Mom, I need to go with you. But I don't know what to say to Brandon's folks. How about you, Pete, are you going or do you want to stay here?"

"I'll go. Let me run upstairs and change clothes and we will all go over." Pete came down a few minutes later in jeans and a polo shirt. "Abby, do you want to ride with me. Mom and dad may want to come home sooner than we do so we better take two cars."

"That's a good idea Pete. Why don't you swing by the club and bring a tray of the finger sandwiches over. When Karen called the club she told them we were going to pick up one tray of the sandwiches so they will have them ready for you. I am sure there will be a crowd at the Millers and people always eat when they are stressed. Abby, honey, are you ok? Are you sure you want to go over there?"

"Barely, I just can't believe this. God, I feel so sorry for Brandon's family. Emily and Jarod idolized their big brother. I don't know what to say to any of them, but I need to go to them. We will be there as soon as we can." As Abby ran upstairs to get some shoes, Abby's mom thanked everyone for coming and told them that they were going to Brandon's house. Slowly people got up, said their goodbyes and drifted out to their cars and drove off. Pete helped Abby into his car, trying not to look at the tears streaming down her face. He swallowed hard to try to clear the baseball sized lump in his throat as he backed out of the driveway. Pete and Abby, both lost in their thoughts, were quiet on the way to the club. Pete pulled up to the back door of the club and one of the waiters who had been watching for them came out carrying a huge tray covered with plastic wrap. Pete got out and opened the back door for him to sit the tray on the back seat. Abby, though all of that, sat with her head bowed unable to look at the club where the wedding reception should have been taking place. Pete couldn't help but think that the parking lot should be filled with happy wedding guests celebrating the marriage of Abby and Brandon, instead of being nearly empty. There were big white bows tied all along the fence leading to the clubhouse that Abby and her mother had placed there earlier as a festive way to welcome the guests to the reception. Now they just added to the sadness of the day. Abby closed her eyes and wouldn't look at them.

Chapter Four

A little over an hour later, Jack and Jerry walked into the police station. The dispatcher motioned them over and said the chief had called an emergency meeting regarding the shooting at the church. Jack and Jerry walked down the hall and stepped into the auditorium type conference room where their fellow officers were getting briefed about the shooting. The room was nearly full, so they quietly took seats in the back of the room. Chief Bruin looked up as they came in and nodded at them. He had just begun speaking and he was outlining the chain of events from the shooting at the church. The three fatalities had been transported to the morgue and three injured parties had been taken to Memorial City Hospital, two others had been treated at the scene. They had twenty to twenty-five prints from the bell tower that they were running through CODIS. On Monday, they would fingerprint the church staff and maintenance people to eliminate anyone who had a legitimate reason for being in the bell tower and see who was left. They had not found any casings in the bell tower or on the property. Interviews with the wedding guests and the neighbors hadn't provided any further information except for the mention of the old red truck. Chief Bruin looked up at Jack and Jerry and asked "You guys were at the wedding. Do you have anything to add?"
Both men regretfully shook their heads no.

"OK, to summarize, we have three dead, three hospitalized and two others slightly injured. We don't know if the shooter was shooting randomly or if he had a particular target or targets in mind. We don't know if there was one shooter or more, won't know that till the autopsies come back and we recover as many bullets as we can find out in the courtyard. We don't know how or when he entered or exited the church. We know he probably had a high powered sniper rifle and he was an excellent shot because each of the three victims was killed with one well-placed shot. I've left a team at the church in case anyone tries to come back for the weapon if he left it there. Tomorrow, I want a couple of teams back in the neighborhood to question all of the neighbors again. When it's daylight, I want another team back at the church to try and find the bullets that passed through the victims. Take metal detectors and go over the grounds foot by foot. Be careful out there. Keep your eyes open. That's all for now."

Chairs scrapped the floor and snatches of conversation were heard as the officers got up and slowly filed out. Several of the officers and detectives nodded at Jack and Jerry and three or four of them slapped the men on the back as they filed past. Ginny McIntyre detoured around some of the officers and came up to Jack and Jerry, giving each of them a quick hug. "Guys, I am so sorry about what happened. I know you were tight with Brandon. What an awful thing to have happen on their wedding day. How's Abby holding up?"

"She's at home, Pete's with her. I think she is still in shock. I know I'm still in shock." Jack said.

"Me, too. It all happened so fast." Jerry replied.

Ginny patted the two men on their arms and walked out with the two teams that were going to canvass the neighborhood tomorrow. Most of the officers were going to try to get some rest before they came back tomorrow.

"So what do we do now, Jerry? We are off duty till Monday." "Let's drive by the church, we have to pick up Brandon's SUV anyway and get it cleaned up before we take it to Brandon's house. Maybe then we will drive through the neighborhood; something might come to us. I sure don't want to go home and I can't face Abby again right now." Jack said.

"I know. God, why Brandon? I can't believe today. I keep hearing those shots and seeing Brandon fall to the ground. I didn't realize anyone else was shot until after the shooting stopped."

Chapter Five

Friday, April 13, 2007

They held the funeral services for Brandon the following Friday afternoon. The chapel was packed with family, co-workers and friends. Jack looked around the beautiful old church and saw many of the same people he had seen at the wedding the preceding Saturday. Everyone in the church was remembering the terror they went through when the shooting started. Jack's parents were sitting in the second pew with Jerry's parents. Jack was standing with Jerry and the rest of the pallbearers when he saw Abby and her parents come down the aisle. Abby and Karen were each clutching one of Ted's arms. The three of them stumbled down the aisle toward the front of the church. Abby's slim black dress hung on her gaunt frame. Her face was pale and drawn and there were dark circles under her eyes. She was clutching a handful of tissues and Jack could see she was struggling not to fall apart. Brandon's parents were sitting across the aisle with Emily and Jarod. Emily and Susan were crying and holding on to each other. They looked up at Abby as she walked toward them. Susan stood up and hugged Abby and Carol before Abby sat down across from them. Jarod sat between his dad and his sister, trying not to cry. Bob sat stiffly at the other end of the pew, his face a grim mask. Jack saw Bob slip his arm around Jarod, and Jarod lean into his father's embrace.

The organist began playing softly the opening bars of "How Great Thou Art" and Millie Blackburn came out and began to sing. The six pallbearers filed in and sat in the first row of the chapel. The rest of the service went by in a blur. Jack clenched his teeth and kept his eyes on the casket trying to ignore the tears that threatened to fall. He knew if they ever got started, they would be difficult to stop. Finally, the minister motioned to the pallbearers that it was time to carry the casket outside. The six pallbearers gently picked up the casket and carried it out to the hearse and slid it inside. A light rain began falling as the first of the limousines pulled out of the church parking lot heading toward the grave site. *Even the heavens were weeping on this sad day*, Jack thought. Jack and Jerry and both sets of their parents rode in the limousine directly behind the two limousines carrying Brandon's family and Abby and her parents. Police were stopping the traffic at the light so the long, sad stream of limos and cars could exit the church and make their way to the cemetery. The procession of cars and limos turned down the tree lined drive and came to a stop a few yards from an open grave covered by a large tent. The rain continued to fall as they gathered around the grave site. Underneath the tent the funeral home had set up rows of chairs. A couple of dozen people crowded together to stand under the shelter of the tent behind the rows of folding chairs, but many more were standing in the rain. Thankfully, the minister kept the grave side service short and after the service everyone filed past the casket and laid a single white Gerber daisy on it before they made their way back to their cars. Gerber daisies in magenta, pink and white were Abby's flower of choice for the wedding and somehow it seemed fitting to hand them out at Brandon's funeral.

Jack, numb with grief, rode with his parents back to Brandon's house. He saw Abby and Pete pull up with their parents. Abby and her family waited on the curb until Jack and his parents caught up with them. One by one each of them hugged the others before they turned and walked slowly up the walk to Brandon's house. Susan looked up as they came in and made her way across the crowded room to hug Jack and his parents. She could barely look at Abby's pain filled face, but she held out her arms and the two of them clung to each other, sharing their grief. Susan and Bob had been thrilled, but not surprised when Abby and Brandon got engaged. Abby had never dated anyone but Brandon and vice versa. They had always loved Abby like their own daughter. Jared and Emily stood back, not quite knowing what to do with themselves, finally coming over and Abby hugged each of them. Everyone was still talking about the unlikely shooting at the church and no one could understand why the police hadn't found out who did the shooting. Jack tried to explain that there wasn't any evidence to link to anyone and until they found a weapon that matched the bullets they had recovered from the scene or some hard physical evidence, they had no where to look. In situations like this, people always wanted answers, but sometimes there just weren't any.

Chapter Six

Monday, April 30, 2007, 6:43 a.m.

Jack was having coffee and reading the paper at his kitchen table when the phone rang. His pulse rate increased when he saw it was the station. "This is Jack."

"All off duty police officers and detectives are requested to report to the station as soon as possible. Sniper fire has been reported on Katy Freeway at Blalock." Jack experienced a pang of grief so intense that nearly immobilized him from the memory of Brandon lying dead on the ground. Jack shook his head to rid himself of the memory, grabbed his keys and ran out the door. It was a madhouse at the station. The duty officer was handing out Kevlar vests and assault rifles. Some of the officers were being issued the bulletproof hoods with clear visors. Jack supposed they would be assigned to check out the vehicles on I-10 and possibly be in more danger than the other officers because of their being out in the open. As Jack suited up and pulled on his Kevlar vest and black windbreaker with "Police" written in big white letters on the back, more and more officers were arriving. He saw Jerry come in and look over at him. Jerry motioned to him to hold up a minute. Jerry jerked on his gear and walked over to Jack.

"Man, this really sucks. Another damn shooting. I haven't come to terms with the last shooting yet." Jerry said as he pulled on the lightweight windbreaker over his vest. "It's going to be hotter than hell in these vests and jackets."

As everyone was suiting up, the duty officer told them there was sniper fire and that there were at least four people killed in their vehicles that they knew of and he didn't know how many were injured. The officers and detectives were given their assignments as they hurried out the door. Jack and Jerry ran out to their car. They, along with four uniformed officers, were to check out two buildings that faced the freeway with their adjacent parking lots on the south side of the freeway between Echo Lane and Campbell. The freeway was at a standstill. Victims had spun out of control when they were shot and careened into other vehicles. Other vehicles in turn had either swerved to avoid being hit and hit other vehicles or ran into the guardrails. Many of the drivers had driven down the embankment to try to reach the feeder road and vacate the area, which caused a major backup on the feeder road. News and police helicopters were circling overhead like noisy vultures, each vying for a better shot of the action. Uniformed officers were using bullhorns to tell people to stay in their cars and to stay down but still some people were getting out of their cars trying to see what was holding up traffic. The shooting had stopped ten minutes ago but no one knew when or if it might start up again. There were numerous buildings with parking garages facing the freeway and every building had to be checked out. Officers with binoculars were scanning the rooftops and parking garages trying to see if they could spot the sniper. They could see people looking out the windows, but didn't see anyone with a rifle. Some people were in the parking garages looking down on the freeway. Officers were trying to keep people from leaving the parking lots and garages, but weren't having much luck at it. There were just too many exits.

JUDY KAY

Jack and Jerry checked out the dusty parking lot beside the first building. They looked into, between and under each of the cars in the parking lot in front of the building and then they went into the building. The building was a two story office building with offices opening off both sides of a long hallway. There were elevators just as you entered the building, but Jack and Jerry took the stairs at the end of the hallway to the top floor. Two uniformed officers were checking the offices on the ground floor and the other two were watching the stairwells and the elevators to make sure no one left the building. Jack and Jerry worked their way through the offices on the second floor warning the people inside to get down on the floor away from the windows. No one heeded their warnings, as they continued to look out the windows at the backed up freeway and the helicopters circling overhead. Even inside the building Jack and Jerry could hear the whomp whomp of the helicopters and the cacophony of cars honking and the bullhorns blasting. The people staring out the window were mesmerized by the chaos outside. The two men saw the door to the roof at the same time.

"Come on, let's check it out." Jack said as they ran toward the door. There was a sign on the door stating that an alarm would go off if the door was opened. To preserve fingerprints if there were any, Jack used his elbow to push the bar down on the door and push the door open. He went through high and Jerry went through low as they had been taught. No alarm sounded and the stairwell was empty. Jack looked at Jerry and they both thought the same thing. Either the alarm was broken or someone had disabled it and whoever it was could still be up there. Jerry leaned over the railing and looked down the stairwell but didn't see anyone. He motioned up with his thumb. They ran up the stairs as quietly and as quickly as they could and pushed the door to the roof open, once again going through in the high and low position. They ducked out quickly looking around. The roof was empty and hot in the early morning sun; the gravel and tar paper roof dusty under their feet. In the center of the roof, there were six large air conditioning units humming in the early morning heat. They checked around and between the units and then they walked toward the freeway side of the building, looking down at the traffic mess on I-10. They walked the length of the roof looking for shell casings or anything else out of place. Three quarters around the roof, they found a fire escape on the south side of the building away from the freeway. On each of the top two steps they could see a dusty footstep. The prints had to be from today because it had rained yesterday, but they had no way of knowing to whom the footprints might have belonged. They followed the fire escape down into the alley, being careful not to touch the railing and not to step on the dusty prints. There were more dusty footprints on the bottom few steps going up the stairs. In the empty alley, there was nothing to tell them if a vehicle had been parked there or which way someone might have gone. Jack was aware that snipers look for areas of opportunity. The only windows on the backside of the building were narrow windows close to the ceiling on the first and second floors and the stairs from the roof led down to the alley. Someone could have come up here with a rifle and not be seen by anyone in the building. Tall trees lined the fence behind the alley, effectively blocking the view from the houses behind the trees. There were two solid doors in the back of the building leading into the alley. Jack tried both doors and they were locked from the inside.

Jerry called the station and told the Sergeant about the footprints they had found. "Keep everyone off the fire escape. I'll send someone to dust for fingerprints on the railing and to get a copy of the footprints. We think the shooter is gone for now, it's been a while since anyone heard a shot. They are shutting down the freeway and diverting traffic to the feeder. It will be a while before they allow the cars to be moved until we can determine for sure the angle for the shooting. That building you just searched is about the right direction for the sniper as far as we can tell. Right now, it looks like the shots were fired from an upper angle down toward the freeway. Don't know if there was one shooter or more. Just like the other damn shooting, no one has found any casings. Nothing to go on yet. None of the other teams have come up with anything at all."

Jack walked the alley looking for anything to connect to the shooter, if in fact, he had come this way. Jerry stayed by the fire escape until the crime team showed up. A few minutes later they came they came roaring up and stopped a few feet from the back stairs. Two of the crime scene members got out of the car and walked over to Jerry. He pointed out the footprints and he suggested they go through the building and come out the fire escape from the roof. "We were careful not to step on the footprints nor touch the railing. We also didn't touch the ledge facing the freeway, in case there are any prints there. I'll stay down here so no one comes up from this direction." Jack walked back to stand with Jerry until the crime crew had done their work.

Traffic officers were beginning to get the traffic moving off the freeway and down onto the feeder road. No one paid any attention to the old red truck chugging along the feeder road. The freeway was closed in both directions and ambulances had taken some of the victims away. Wrecker drivers were beginning to pull out of the long line where they were waiting and starting to tow the cars that had not been shot but had crashed into other vehicles or into the guardrails. Jack watched as they maneuvered their way through the traffic jam to hook up the damaged vehicles. Jack's radio crackled and he pressed the listen button. He learned this time there were five fatalities and four injured people had been taken to Memorial City Hospital. Jack shuddered as though someone had walked on his grave. *First, the shooting at the wedding and now this shooting, what the hell in going on.* Jack thought to himself. They didn't have much of anything from the first shooting. The only real evidence that they had was the 45-70 long range bullets they found outside the church, so they assumed the shooter had used a sniper rifle. There were no fingerprints on the bullets. They weren't able to get a match on any of the fingerprints in the bell tower other than those of church personnel.

After the crime crew finished fingerprinting the railing and lifting a print of the foot marks on the fire escape which might or might not be connected to the freeway shooting, Jack and Jerry headed back to the station.

Chapter Seven

Jack was at the station helping with paperwork on the latest shooting when his cell phone rang. "It's Abby, I just heard about the freeway shooting. Do you think it is the same person who fired the shots at the church?"

Jack could hear the terror in Abby's voice and knew that this shooting had probably brought the tragedy of the wedding shooting crashing down on her the same as it had on him. "Abby, we don't know. Today, there were five fatalities and so far as I know four injured. Looks like the guy used a sniper rifle but we won't know till we either find some casings or some of the bullets. I'll keep you posted. Do you feel like grabbing a bite to eat tonight? I should be finished here around 5:00 o'clock"

"I suppose so. I'm not very hungry these days."

"It's going to take a while, Abby. We are all still in a state of shock. Ask Pete if he wants to join us, we can grab a burger at Pappa's Burgers and watch the Astros. Roy Oswalt is pitching tonight. I'll ask Jerry if he and Kristen want to join us."

"Ok. I will check with him when he gets off his shift. What time are you going to pick us up?"

"I'll be there around 6:30 p.m. That will give me time to shower and change before I pick you up." Jack hung up the phone. "Hey Jerry, we're going to Pappa's for burgers and to watch the Astros, do you and Kristen want to join us?"

"I'll call her and let you know. Sounds good. We haven't seen much of Abby and Pete since..." Jerry couldn't bear to finish the sentence. Jack was glad Abby had agreed to go out for a bite. He knew she hadn't been out of the house since the funeral and Carol had said she was barely eating. The last time he had seen her, she looked like she had lost more weight and she was already skin and bones.

Jack showered and put on his Astros's jersey with his well worn jeans. Abby and Pete must have been watching for him as they came out the door as he drove up. Carol waved at him from the window. Pete held the door and Abby scrambled in the back of the SUV and Pete got in front.

Pete asked about the freeway shooting and Jack repeated what little he knew. Glancing back at Abby, Pete abruptly changed the subject, realizing that talking about another shooting probably would be too hard on her.

When they pulled in the parking lot, they saw Jerry's truck. "Looks like Jerry and Kristen beat us here. I hope they got a good table." As usual, Pappa's was crowded with avid sports fans. They saw Jerry and Kristen at a table directly in front of one of the huge wide screen televisions showing the pre-game. They grinned at them as they joined the table. Jerry and Kristen had a beer in front of them and after the waiter had taken the drink orders for Abby, Pete and Jack they all hugged and started to catch up on what was happening in their lives, being careful not to mention Brandon. All of a sudden, tears started running down Abby's face and she jumped up and ran to the restroom. Kristen got up and followed her.

The men just looked at each other. They were all feeling Brandon's absence and it was so much worse on Abby. This was the first time they had got together without him. The waiter brought their drinks and took their order for burger platters all around. A few minutes later, Kristen and Abby came back to the table, their eyes red from crying. The men tried not to look at them and when their burgers came they tried to distract the women by arguing over whether Oswalt was a better pitcher than Nolan Ryan had been in his heyday. Jack was glad to see that Abby ate all of her burger and picked at a few of the fries. While Abby was engrossed in the game, Jack quietly studied her. She still had dark circles under her eyes and she was awfully thin. Her movements were herky-jerky as though she had too much caffeine in her system. He could tell she wasn't sleeping much. Pete and Jerry looked nearly as bad as Abby. Pete was pale and he also had dark circles under his eyes. He noticed how badly Pete's hands were shaking when he picked up his beer. Jack hoped all of them would start to heal from their loss. Though they didn't mention Brandon, they all felt the emptiness of him not being with them. It just didn't feel right without Brandon sitting beside Abby. They were far more subdued than normal while watching the game. Normally, they would have been shouting and cheering loudly when the Astros scored or made a good play and jeering at the other team, but there wasn't much of that going on tonight. The Astros won 8 to 5. They drank a victory beer and got up to leave. Out in the parking lot, they just hugged each other and Jack could see the sheen of tears in Abby's and Kristen's eyes.

Abby and Pete got out of the SUV at their house. Abby came around to Jack's side of the SUV and opened the door to hug him. "Thanks for getting me out of the house. It was hard but I need to start putting my life back together." Tears started streaming down her face as she turned back to Pete and Jack watched them as Pete draped his arm around Abby and they slowly walked up the sidewalk and into the house.

Jack drove back to his apartment feeling lonely and blue. He was having a hard time coming to grips with the fact that

Brandon was no longer there. Every time something funny happened, he would catch himself picking up his cell phone to call Brandon and tell him about it. Abby and Pete had each other to lean on and Jerry had Kristen. He had put on a good face for Abby and Pete, but since Brandon's death, he felt like a part of him was missing. The five of them had been so close, but it always seemed to Jack that Brandon was the brother he never had. Brandon was Pete's age, a year older than Abby, Jack and Jerry. He could tell Brandon anything. Brandon would always listen and not say much. If he offered any advice at all, it was usually good advice. He especially missed Brandon's wicked sense of humor and his practical jokes. He wished that they would find the sniper, so he could put that part to rest. Jack still avoided driving by the church whenever he could. It worried him that so soon after the shooting at the church, there was this shooting on the freeway. He hoped it wouldn't turn out to be some lunatic taking potshots all over town or worse, a copycat of the Virginia shootings that had gone on for weeks before they finally caught the snipers.

Chapter Eight
May 13, 2007

"911, what's your emergency?"

"I'm on Westheimer in front of the Galleria and I think there are shots being fired. Oh damn, that one was close."

"Where on Westheimer are you? What's the cross street?"

"Post Oak. Oh no, I see two pedestrians who have been shot and someone is shooting at the cars. Those two pedestrians aren't moving, oh my God, I think they are dead."

"Please, stay on the line, I am notifying officers of the situation. Ma'am, Ma'am, are you there? Please respond, Ma'am?" Just then the 911 operator heard glass breaking and a loud crash. In the background, she could hear horns honking and people screaming.

Jack and Jerry were doing a follow-up interview for a liquor store robbery on Sage when they heard the request for officers to respond to a shooting at the Galleria. Looking at each other in panic, they rushed out to their car and headed toward Westheimer with siren and lights blazing. Traffic was horrendous with people trying to flee the Galleria area and others were trying to see what was happening. They tried to make their way toward Chimney Rock but Westheimer was at a standstill. Jack whipped the car into a parking lot in front of FAO Schwartz and they got out of the car and made their way through the panicked crowd on foot. They could see at least five wrecked cars and several cars looked like they were abandoned. They saw two pedestrians who had been shot and people were standing around gawking at the sight. Jack and Jerry were scanning rooftops and parking garages as they ran toward Chimney Rock. People were standing around on the sidewalks taking pictures with their cell phones. Police were trying to get the traffic moving and other officers were trying to herd bystanders into stores to get them out of sight.

"Get inside, please, shots have been fired. Everyone get inside right now." Jack shouted as he ran up. He thought he caught a glimpse of muzzle fire from the roof of the parking garage across the street. He stepped behind a sign and heard another shot. He chanced a glance around the sign but didn't see anything else. Jerry was running across the street and trying to get to the parking garage. Jack took off after him. There were several exits to the parking garage. Jack called to two of the officers on the scene and told them to try and stop all traffic coming out the Westheimer side. They ran around toward the next exit and could see a long line of vehicles slowly making their way out of the garage. They knew there wasn't any way to get them stopped and search every vehicle. Besides the two exits on the Westheimer side, there were two exits on two other sides of the parking garage. Many vehicles had already exited the garage. They certainly couldn't make a list of all the license numbers and it wouldn't do any good anyway. The shooter could simply put his rifle in the trunk of his car and walk into the Galleria and come back later for his car. They turned back toward the Westheimer exit and saw the patrolmen weren't able to stop people from leaving the garage from that exit either. Several cars nearly hit the officers as they tried to get their vehicles out of the garage. Everyone was in a panic trying to flee the area.

It had been about twelve minutes since Jack had heard the last shot fired. Whoever the sniper was, he was probably long gone. It would take hours to sort out the traffic problems and remove the damaged vehicles. Ambulances and wreckers were beginning to pull into the area, guided through the traffic by the police on the scene. Jack and Jerry saw at least seven dead and four injured. Two of the dead were pedestrians shot on the sidewalk, the rest had been shot in their cars. Many of the wounds were through and through meaning the sniper had probably used a high powered rifle just like the other shootings. Jerry thought they probably wouldn't get any more than they had in the past shootings. Different guns had been used in each of the first two shootings, both of which were probably high powered rifles judging by the spent bullets they had found. Other than that, they weren't any closer to catching the sniper or snipers. If they did get him or them, it would be pure damn luck. Jerry shook his head with disgust.

"Let's see if we can help get this mess cleared up and then let's go grab some lunch." Jack said. They started interviewing people who were stopped in the cars around the wrecked vehicles. No one could tell them how many shots had been fired, where the shots had came from and they hadn't seen anyone shooting. It was the same story as the other shootings. Whoever this guy or guys were, they were like ghosts. They just appeared and disappeared just as quickly. There were approximately fifty officers and detectives on site. There would be hundreds of interviews and probably nothing conclusive again. Civilians couldn't understand why the shooter hadn't been caught. News stations were crucifying the police because they didn't have a suspect yet. Drivers can't prepare for a sniper randomly shooting at them. Houston, at nearly 600 square miles, the fourth largest U.S. city in terms of land area and no way to know where and when a sniper would strike next was daunting and scary to everyone, most of all the police. That evening Jack was listening to the news about the shooting. "The Houston Sniper is killing people at random, firing a single bullet in each victim, firing from as far as 100 yards away. There is nothing a civilian can do to protect himself or herself from these random shootings. Let's hope the police get this sniper or snipers soon. No one is safe from something like this." The news anchor ended his commentary and Jack shook his head as he switched off the television.

Chapter Nine

May 17, 2007

Jack looked at the duty roster and noticed that he had the coming Saturday off. He really needed to get away and the beach had always soothed him. He picked up the phone and called Abby. "What are you doing?"

"Just trying to read an article. Can't make much sense of it though, I keep reading the same paragraph over and over."

I've got Saturday off, do you want to drive down to Galveston to the beach?"

"OK, I guess." Abby said without much enthusiasm.

"That doesn't sound very positive, come on, it will do you good to get outside and get some sunshine. Do you know if Pete has to work?"

"No, but he is helping Tony move on Saturday. OK, I'll pack a cooler with some drinks. Maybe we will have lunch or an early dinner somewhere on the Strand. You're right, Jack, I do need to get out of the house. It's so hard to force myself to go anywhere though. I feel like I am going through the motions of living, but not quite making it."

"I know. Me too. I go to work and then back to my apartment. I watch TV but it doesn't register. Then all these damn shootings. We aren't getting anywhere with that. It is so frustrating. There is just nothing to go on. It's like this guy is a puff of smoke. We are spinning our wheels with the investigation." Jack said.

"Don't you think they must be connected?"

"I think they are probably connected, but we don't have anything to link the shootings together. It's strange to me that not one person has spotted the sniper."

"I hope that when they catch this sniper or snipers, it will help me cope with everything. I feel so lost without Brandon. It's like my heart has been ripped out of me. Some days it is all I can do to get out of bed and get dressed." Abby said.

"I sure understand that, I feel like I am missing a part of myself as well. It will do us both good to get out of town for a day. I'll pick you up around 10:00." Jack smiled as he hung up. Abby had always loved the beach. They all had. He remembered one time when they were 16 or 17 years old and all of them had gone to the beach one Saturday. Abby went to the public bathroom to change into her swimsuit and while she was gone, Brandon dug a hole, laid down in it and had them cover him with sand. He put a short straw in his mouth so he could breathe and they had smoothed the sand over him so you couldn't tell he was there. He, Pete and Jerry were laughing and cutting up when Abby came back and spread out her towel then sat down on it. She was about a foot from where Brandon was buried.

"Where's Brandon" she asked as she looked around. Just then Brandon came screaming out of the sand like some monster from a horror movie. Abby had screamed so loud and when she jumped up, she peed down her leg. They had all laughed themselves sick. They never let her forget it. They were always horsing around and playing practical jokes on each other. That was another thing he missed about Brandon, all the laughter and the fun. He felt like he hadn't laughed since Brandon was shot.

51

Saturday, May 19, 2007

Saturday morning Jack got up early and went for a run in Memorial Park. He came home and put a pot of coffee on and jumped in the shower. After he drank his coffee, he gathered up the items he wanted to take to the beach with him. He came out of his apartment wearing his swim trunks and a tee shirt and carrying a large beach umbrella and a tote with some clean clothes and his beach towel. He went back inside and brought out two chaise lounges. He tried to think if he was forgetting anything, but decided he wasn't. It was really going to be hot today. There wasn't a cloud in the sky and it must be 90° already and it was just 10:00 o'clock. Sweat ran in rivulets down Jack's back as he loaded the car. Of course, in Houston, it was always hot and humid in the summer, he should be used to it by now. He pulled up in front of Abby's house and she came out. She was so cute in her big floppy hat and sunglasses, he had to smile. She had a small cooler and her beach tote which she threw in the backseat before climbing in beside Jack. She smiled a little sad smile and said with a hitch in her voice "This is the first time I've been to the beach this year."

"Me, too. In fact, it is the first time I've been out of town since Brandon died." Jack said as he pulled out. They talked about the Astros, the weather and other things, carefully avoiding any further mention of Brandon or the shootings. Before they knew it, they were on the seawall. It was a beautiful sunny day and the water was as blue as Jack had ever seen it. As usual, the beach was starting to get crowded already. Families were setting up umbrellas and kids were kicking water at each other. Colorful chaise lounges and beach chairs dotted the beach. Big beach umbrellas were catching the gentle sea breezes. Jack found a parking place close to the stairs. He got out, opened up the back hatch and pulled the chaise lounges out.

"Boy, you thought of everything, Jack." Abby said as she grabbed her tote and the cooler. "Do you want me to carry anything?"

"No, if you can take the cooler and your tote, I can manage the rest." Jack put his tote over his shoulder, stuck the umbrella under his arm and picked up the chaise lounges. "Let's try to find someplace close to the bottom of the stairs. I don't know how far I can carry all of this stuff."

"It looks like we are moving in for the week. Funny, how much stuff you need for an afternoon at the beach." Abby laughed as she walked down the stairs to the beach, her flip flops kicking up little clouds of sand with each step.

They got to the bottom of the stairs and set their stuff down. Jack set up the chaise lounges and anchored the big umbrella in the sand. Abby opened the cooler and handed Jack a coke. She laughed at the wry look he gave it. "Remember Jack, no alcohol on the beach. You wouldn't want to get arrested for drinking on the beach. Think how embarrassing that would be!"

Abby slipped off her red gauzy beach cover-up and ran down to the water. Jack held back and admired her in the cute little red bikini. She was still too thin but at least for now she looked a little happier. He gave her a little head start then caught up with her and dunked her in the water. She came up laughing and spluttering salt water and splashed him. It brought back happy memories for both of them, when the five of them would come to the beach as kids. Each day brought a little healing from the grief and the laughter was coming easier now.

"Do you remember when you guys were all horsing around in the water and you held Pete down and took his swim trunks off and brought them up to the edge of the seawall?" Abby laughed.

"Oh boy, do I. We were sitting up here laughing our asses off because he couldn't get out of the water. He must have stayed in the water for an hour shouting at us to bring his trunks back to him. Finally he came tearing out of the water and grabbed his trunks and ran back in the water to put them on. I never will forget the look on those two girls' faces when he streaked across the beach!" Jack and Abby both laughed at the memory. "Too bad he had to help Tony move today. He could have used a day away also."

They walked along the edge of the water, close but not touching, laughing at dogs fetching balls and chasing seagulls in the water, smiling at children playing and admiring the sand castles they were building. Every once in a while a bigger wave would come rolling in and splash them up to their waists. They would laugh and try to get out of the way of the wave. They smiled at each other, both enjoying the beautiful day. They pointed out pretty shells, but didn't pick any up. When you lived close to the beach there wasn't any reason to drag shells home with you. They left the shelling to the tourists. Jack bought them strawberry snow cones from a vendor on the beach and then they rented a bicycle built for two and rode a couple of miles down the beach and back.

After they turned in the bicycle, they walked back to their chaise lounges and sat facing the water. Abby asked Jack to take the umbrella down as she wanted to get a little sun. After a while, Jack noticed that Abby's eyes slowly drifted shut. He was glad to see she was able to relax and sleep a little. He knew she hadn't been sleeping much since Brandon was shot. He sat watching her as she slept and thought about how precious she was to him. He realized that he was in love with her and had been for a long time. He had tamped down his feelings and hidden them in a corner of his heart while Brandon had been alive because he knew Abby loved Brandon and always had, but now he couldn't hide his feelings from himself any longer. It was too soon for Abby to know how he felt, he would continue to be supportive and a friend until the time was right. *Brandon, old buddy, you always knew what was in my heart, I hope you will understand, I know you would want Abby to be happy and I will do everything in my power to give her that happiness.* Jack thought to himself. As he sat there, a weight lifted from his heart just knowing that there might be a chance for them. He knew Brandon wouldn't want Abby to stop living just because he had. Jack hoped Abby would get to the point where she no longer thought of him as another brother, but if she didn't then he would have to be satisfied with just being her friend. He let Abby sleep for an hour or so and then he noticed that her fair skin was starting to get sunburned. He put his hand on her arm and gave her a little shake.

"What?" She said as she woke up. "Did I fall asleep?"

"Yeah, and you were snoring and drooling down your chin. Three kids came by and took pictures of you with their cell phones because you looked so funny. I woke you up before you could embarrass yourself anymore."

"Oh, you jerk. I do not snore and I certainly don't drool."

Jack laughed. "Maybe you're right, it might have been slobber instead of a drool!"

"Jack, you are an idiot!" she laughed and he delighted in the sound. He hadn't heard her laugh very much since the shooting.

"Hey, I'm getting hungry. Why don't we go change clothes and grab a bite to eat on the Strand."

"You are always hungry. OK, I'm ready." They gathered up their belongings and walked up the steps and back to the car. A little ways down the beach there were public restrooms with showers where they could change. Jack finished first and was waiting outside the restrooms when Abby came out a few minutes later. She had showered and washed her hair but not dried it, just tied it with a yellow ribbon. She never wore much makeup and now she just had on lipstick and mascara and of course, her big floppy hat. She had changed into cute little yellow shorts and had tied her shirt in a knot leaving a couple inches of bare skin showing at her tiny waist. She looked like she was sixteen again. *If only they could go back to those happier times.*

Jack whistled when she came out. "You look cute." he said.

She grinned at him and then sobered quickly. "You know, for a while, I wasn't thinking about Brandon."

"Abby, you know Brandon wouldn't want you to go through life never laughing again. He loved it when you laughed. Don't feel guilty because we are having a little fun. He will always be in our hearts. We won't ever forget him and we will carry a piece of him with us forever."

Abby slipped her hand in his as they walked back to the car. They were quiet as they drove to the Strand. Jack found a parking space close to Colonel Bubbie's and they walked along window shopping, both lost in their own thoughts, finally stopping at Rudy and Pacco's for an early dinner. Jack had a beer and Abby had a glass of wine. They ordered the fish tacos and munched on chips and salsa until their meals came. They didn't talk much through dinner, it seemed like their energy had drained as the sun went down. After they finished eating, they walked back to the car and started back to Houston. They were quiet on the way back, but it wasn't an uncomfortable silence, both seemed lost in their memories. When they got to the Galleria right before the 610 interchange with Katy Freeway traffic was backed up horribly. "What the hell is this? Traffic shouldn't be this bad this time of day on a Saturday." Jack asked out loud.

He tried to switch lanes and get off at Woodway, but nothing was moving. He switched the radio on just as the radio announcer broke into the programming. "This is an emergency notice. Sniper fire has been reported on the Katy Freeway at the 610 interchange. If you hear this announcement and are in the vicinity, please vacate the area immediately if you are able to do so. Repeat, vacate the area immediately. If you are unable to move your vehicle, please stay in your cars and get down as low as you possibly can. I repeat, sniper fire at Katy Freeway and 610 Loop. Stay tuned for more details." Jack looked at Abby and shook his head.

"Oh no, not again." She cried.

"Abby, lay your seat back and get down as low as you can. I'll try to get us out of here."

Abby laid her seat back as far as possible and got down as far as she could. Jack slid down in the seat until he could just see over the dashboard to steer the car. Jack heard the police and news helicopters thump, thump, thumping overhead and heard sirens screaming from all directions. Jack could see people driving down the embankments and honking their horns trying to get other vehicles to move out of their way. Finally, the car to the right of Jack drove down the embankment and Jack whipped his SUV over two lanes amid mad honking and slipped and slid down the embankment onto the feeder road. He hooked a right on Memorial which was the first street he came to and took off as fast as he could. He could see other vehicles following him down the embankment and onto Memorial. Abby pulled her seat back upright was sitting beside him in shock, her eyes as big as saucers, and her face white with fear. When they were a little ways down Memorial and away from the worst of the traffic, he pulled over and took her in his arms. Other cars were stopping and people were getting out of their vehicles. Abby sagged against him and he could feel her shaking and her tears soaking through his shirt. He held her close until she stopped shaking.

"Abby, are you ok?"

"Yes. I guess so. I was so scared back there. It brings back the horror of the shooting at the wedding. I had a flashback where I saw the blood coming out of Brandon's chest and him collapsing on the ground. I thought I was going to throw up, it was so real. Do you think this is the same sniper or snipers from the church and the other incidents?"

"It probably is. I would hate to think that we have copycat snipers. Something or someone has got this guy or guys wound up. There doesn't seem to be any rhyme or reason as to where or when he will strike again. I need to get you home and then I need to go to the station and check in." He held her away from him and looked at her tear-stained face. "You sure you're ok? You're so pale."

"It just brings back the horror of Brandon being shot when I hear about another shooting. I'll be ok as soon as I get home." Jack took a left down to Westheimer and drove her home as quickly as he could. Abby jumped out and grabbed the cooler and her tote. "Call me later when you know something about this latest shooting. I had fun before that happened. Bye." Abby said as she closed the door and ran up the steps. She stopped and waved before she went inside.

Chapter Ten

It was an absolute madhouse at the police station. They had confirmed five dead, two of which were in one vehicle and at least six more people injured by gunshot. The gunshot victims had been taken to the hospital. Some of the other injuries were caused when vehicles plowed into them trying to avoid hitting another car in front of them. Once again, they had to close the freeway down while they looked for shell casings and bullets. Crime scene investigators were going over the victims and their cars trying to determine from what angle the shots had been fired. They had gotten all the other vehicles off the freeway except for those which had been hit by bullets but the freeway was still shut down. The wrecker trucks were lined up like vultures waiting to tow off the wrecked cars. There were teams of officers canvassing the neighboring buildings where a sniper might have been. It was a difficult situation since it was a Saturday evening and many of the businesses were closed. The buildings which had security could be accessed but if there was no security, there was no way to get inside or up to the roof. However, if the buildings had security, the shooter would probably show up on tape or the security guard would have seen him or them. It was a catch-22 situation. They rationed to themselves that if they couldn't get into the buildings or parking garages, chances are the shooter couldn't either. There were numerous buildings and parking garages where a shooter might have been, plus there were several elevated and wooded areas near the highway from where shots could be fired. No one reported seeing anyone shooting. Traffic was still a nightmare in all directions around the interchange. To make matters worse, cars were stalling out and overheating in the traffic jam.

Jack saw Jerry come running into the station in shorts and a polo shirt. Evidently, he had been off duty as well. The Chief motioned for Jack and Jerry to come into his office. "I know the two of you are off duty, but I am pulling you in right now to help out with the paper work on this latest shooting." All of the shootings had caused an avalanche in paperwork because of the number of witness interviews involved. The Chief handed them stacks of handwritten notes from the officers who had been on the scene. "Take these notes and get them in some kind of order so we can make heads or tails of these interviews. I guess put them in alpha order by officers and then in chronological order. We are going to have a briefing in an hour and then we will have to give a statement to the news so they can run it on the 10 o'clock news. I'm hoping that this time we will get something worthwhile out of these interviews. We have to control the panic this latest shooting is sure to invoke. I wish to hell we would get a break in these shootings. The press is really starting to hammer us because we haven't caught him or them yet. Get typing."

Jack and Jerry took the scribbled pages into the conference room and spread them out on the table trying to put them in some semblance of order. From the notes, it looked like the shooting started around 8:19 p.m. The last reported shot was at 8:25, 6 minutes later. Of course, the timing could be off by two or three minutes because people's watches had different time. The first officers on the scene arrived at 8:27. Jack and Jerry quickly sorted the notes and each took half. They sat down at their computers and began typing. Officers began slowly coming back to the station, hot and tired and thirsty. Jack heard one of them cursing because the coke machine was out of cold drinks. It was still 90° outside. The Chief came out and brought them more notes. "I am calling a meeting in 30 minutes in the squad room. Get as much done as you can and print it out for me."

They nodded and kept on typing. Both were proficient on the computer and they were making good headway on the notes even though a lot of the handwriting was hard to decipher. The Chief came by on his way to the meeting and gave them the rest of the notes. "Print out what you have finished. You guys keep on putting these notes into the system. I'm going to go ahead with the meeting on what we have right now, which isn't much. Danelle is working up a press release that we will give to the news teams after this meeting. Thanks for your help on this damn paperwork."

Jack finished the last of his notes and noticed that Jerry only had a few left to type. Jack walked over to the vending machine, then remembered that it was empty. He turned to the coffee pot and poured two cups of the thick black sludge that passed as coffee. It smelled scorched and was probably strong enough to stand on its own. He put lots of cream and sugar in both cups and handed one to Jerry. Jerry finished up and Jack combined his notes with Jerry's and printed out two sets. The horrific shooting incident on the highway was executed with military precision. They both read through the notes and looked up with dismay at each other.

"It still looks like a lot of nothing. No one saw the sniper, no one knows where the shots came from, just like the other shootings. The first indication of anything being wrong was when the first vehicle spun out of control as the driver was killed. The second victim was two cars behind the first, then the two victims in the fifth car. Several motorists reported calling 911 when the vehicles started piling into one another. There were six other gunshot victims who were wounded and four people injured when their cars crashed into vehicles and guardrails. Looks like he or they shot fast and got out of there fast, same as before. Sure not much to go on. I'm anxious to see if the ammunition matches either of the other shootings." Jerry said. The bullets from the first shootings were all fired from different rifles. They still didn't know if it was one sniper with multiple rifles or two or more different snipers. Jack and Jerry started reading witness statements to each other.

One man said that, as he passed beneath an underpass, he heard a gunshot and looked back and saw the car behind him crash into the guardrails. He didn't know what was happening and he looked at his daughter to make sure she was wearing her seatbelt.

Another man testified that he heard "a loud smack" and noticed the windshield of his company car cracking. He thought it might be a rock thrown from an overpass.

A woman said her daughter thought she heard a gunshot right before the driver's window shattered.

A teenager said, "No, I didn't see anything, I was too scared to look. I just wanted to get out of there."

"Well we know the sniper was on the west side of the 610 loop since all of the shots came from that direction. That's why so many drivers were shot."

Jack's cell phone rang and he picked it up. "Hello."

"Hey Jack, it's Abby. What is happening on this latest shooting?"

"Jerry and I are at the station trying to get the interviews typed up for the Chief. It's like the others, same MO, no one saw anything till the vehicles started piling up. Some of the drivers reported hearing gunshots, but couldn't tell where they came from. Most likely they came from that grove of trees on the west side of the freeway. It would be easy for someone to conceal themselves there. They could have parked their vehicle on Memorial and people would have just thought it was someone running in Memorial Park. I still don't understand how they are getting the rifle to these places without someone seeing them."

"I hope you get them soon. This is really getting scary."

"Yeah, I know. The news crews are crucifying us. We just don't have anything to go on."

"I really had fun today, and for a while, I wasn't thinking of Brandon. I have to go now. Talk to you later." Abby hung up the phone as her mother came in the room. Abby looked at her mother and thought how pale she looked. She probably wasn't sleeping any better than Abby was.

"I'm glad you got out of the house today, honey. I know it's hard. It was probably good for Jack to get away also. It's tough on all of you. It takes time to get on with your life. Brandon's death changed all of your lives forever."

Abby stood up and hugged her mother. "Mom, there was another shooting on the freeway today. Jack and I were on the way home from Galveston by the Galleria and we got into the traffic jam caused by the shooting. I was so scared I was nearly sick. Jack drove down the embankment at the 610 Loop and I-10 and got us out of there. More people were killed today. Jack and Jerry are at the station right now dealing with it."

"Oh honey, I hadn't heard about this shooting. I haven't had the TV on all day. I'm so glad you weren't hurt. Thank God,

Jack reacted quickly and got you out of there. He's always watched out for you. I wish to God they would catch this sniper."

"I know mom. I do too. I don't know what I would do without all of you. I couldn't have gotten through Brandon's death without Jack and you and dad and Pete. Thanks for not pressuring me to get out more. I've got to take it one step at a time. Well, I'm tired from my day at the beach and emotionally drained from getting away from the shooting this evening so I think I am going to turn in early. Wake me in the morning so I can go to church with you and dad."

"Nite, honey." Abby's mom said as she watched her go upstairs. Carol was glad Abby had offered to go to church with them in the morning. She hadn't been to church since Brandon was shot. Her heart ached for Abby. She sank down on the couch feeling totally drained. She didn't know why she was so tired all the time, she had done nothing but lay around all day while Abby was at the beach. Maybe it was just stress, she seemed to have gotten worse since Brandon's death. Of course, none of them were sleeping very well these days. She supposed that could be it.

Chapter Eleven

Friday, June 29, 2007

Abby had washed her hair was just getting out of the shower when the phone rang. She wrapped a towel around her hair and grabbed a towel and wrapped herself in it. "Hello" she said breathlessly.

"Abby, it's Jack, you sound out of breath. Are you OK?

"Sure, I just got out of the shower and I wanted to catch the phone before it disturbed mom, she isn't feeling well today."

"I'm sorry to hear that. Tell her hello for me. And what I am calling about is do you want to go the 4th of July Celebration on Allen Parkway? I know you like Montgomery Gentry and they are performing. There are four stages with music ranging from country western and rock 'n' roll to Latin, pop and oldies."

"I guess so. I hadn't made any plans for the 4th. In fact, I hadn't even realized it was nearly July already. I am so out of touch."

"Great, Jerry and I don't have to work, so I thought I would ask Jerry and Kristen if they want to go with us. Is Pete working on the 4th?"

"Yes, Pete has to work. But it sounds like fun to me. What time do you want to go?"

"Let's go about 4:00. We can walk around and people watch and try to scope out a good place to watch the fireworks."

"Ok, I'll see you then."

When Jack stopped in front of Abby's house, he was surprised when she didn't run out as she usually did. He turned off the SUV and walked up to the door. Abby answered the door at his knock. "Come on in, I wanted to make sure mom was comfortable before I left, she still isn't feeling well. Come and say hello to her."

"Hi Carol, Abby said you weren't feeling well. I am sorry to hear that. Anything I can do?" Jack said as he leaned over and kissed her forehead.

"Yes, take this daughter of mine out of here. She fusses over me like I am some little old lady. You kids have fun. I'll be fine. Ted just ran out to the store and he will be home in a few minutes. We plan on watching the celebration on TV. I would love to see the fireworks in person, but I'm sure not up to facing those crowds."

Jack smiled at Carol. He was very fond of her. In spite of her smiling at him, she looked extremely pale and drawn. He hoped it wasn't anything serious. They waved as they went out the front door.

"What's wrong with your mom?" Jack asked when they got in the car.

"I don't know. She hasn't been herself for about two weeks now, well actually, I think it started around the time Brandon was shot. I thought it was just stress, but now I don't know. She has a doctor's appointment on Monday. She hasn't been sleeping well and she is tired all the time. I'm really worried about her and you know how she is, she doesn't want anyone fussing over her."

Jack turned into Kristen's driveway and saw Jerry's truck parked in front of the garage. "Jerry decided to meet us here so we wouldn't have to pick him up." Jerry and Kristen came out of the house laughing and horsing around. They each carried a large beach umbrella.

"You two look like you are in a party mood. What's with the umbrellas? " Abby laughed.

Kristen leaned over the seat to give Abby a hug. "Since it has been raining all week, I thought they might come in handy. If it doesn't rain, they will provide some shade for us. Hey guys, this is going to be fun. Sorry Pete had to work today, I know he would have enjoyed Montgomery Gentry. I've been looking forward to this ever since I heard they were going to be on the big stage. We probably won't be able to get close but with the video screens, it still should be ok and I always love the spectacular fireworks display." Kristen's words always tumbled out of her mouth like a rabid chipmunk. They all got a kick out of her. She was the most enthusiastic person that Abby had ever met. Kristen was always upbeat and tried to see the good in everyone. Jack was glad Kristen was with them, she could cheer anyone up.

Abby looked at Kristen and Jerry and thought that they were perfect for each other. Kristen was a petite blond and Jerry was 6' 2" with coal black hair. Jerry always laughed and said Kristen was so small he could carry her around in his pocket. She wouldn't be surprised if they got engaged before the summer ended. Jerry was the most serious of the five of them and Kristen's bubbling personality was a good match for his quietness. Other than the guys, Kristen was Abby's best friend. She made a note to herself to ask Kristen to lunch soon so they could catch up on what was happening with her. She had barely seen Kristen since Brandon got shot. In fact, she hadn't seen much of anyone. She vowed to be a better friend and stay in contact with Kristen.

Jack found a parking space a few streets away from the Festival. The four of them poured out of the SUV. Jack reached under his seat and grabbed a small drop cloth. Jerry grabbed the umbrellas with one hand and Kristen with the other hand. He stopped to give Kristen a quick kiss before he started toward the festival. The four of them paid their entry fee and started checking out the food stands. "Oh look at those funnel cakes, they are to die for. Who wants to share one with me?" Abby asked.

Jack got a funnel cake and asked for extra powdered sugar. Before he turned around, he pressed his index finger into the sugar. "Here Abby, you get the first bite." Jack said as he handed her the plate. "Wait, you've got something on your nose, let me get it for you." he said as he wiped the tip of her nose with his sugared finger, leaving a huge white smear on her nose.

Jerry and Kristen grinned as they turned away. The people around Abby began grinning at her but she was focused on the funnel cake. Jerry caught Jack's eye and grinned and just shook his head. They walked around stopping to look at booths selling anything and everything imaginable. When they came to a booth selling sunglasses, Abby stopped to try some on. As she looked in the mirror to check out a pair, she noticed the large powdered sugar smudge on her nose. "Oh Jack, you are such a jerk. No wonder everyone was laughing at me. I thought they were just being friendly, but they were laughing at me." She said as she swatted him on the arm and then rubbed the sugar off her nose.

Jack started laughing and then told Jerry and Kristen about Abby falling asleep on the beach and snoring and drooling all over herself. Abby just rolled her eyes at them and kept on walking. Jerry piped up and said he had seen the pictures posted on the internet of Abby sleeping and her mouth was hanging open like a bucket. Kristen slapped both guys and told them to

SHOTS

behave. It was almost like old times with all the joking and kidding around. Jack was glad he had thought of this outing. All the clowning around was helping them get back to normal, if there was such a thing. They walked around watching people and filling up on junk food. Kristen had to have a sausage on a stick. Jack had a turkey leg and Jerry got a big tray of nachos and shared them with the other three. Jack noticed Abby's eyes grew sad as she watched couples walking hand in hand or with their arms around each other. The sun had gone under the clouds and the sky was darkening ominously as the wind started kicking up. Suddenly big fat raindrops began pounding them. The huge rain drops made craters in the dusty ground and loud plopping noises as they hit. Jerry opened his umbrella and Kristen handed hers to Jack. Jack quickly opened the umbrella and Abby stepped into the circle of his arms to get out of the rain. She was standing so close, he could smell the fresh citrus scent of her shampoo. The top of her head came to just under his chin. He tightened his arm around her and stood so he was shielding her from most of the blowing rain. *She fits in my arms just perfect*, Jack thought. The four stood in the shelter of the umbrellas and laughed at people scurrying to get out of the rain. They were all wearing shorts and flip flops so it didn't matter to them if the rain got their feet and legs wet. It had been so hot, the cool stinging rain felt good hitting their legs. They made their way over to where Montgomery Gentry was to perform and found a place to sit and watch the show. Jack unfolded the drop cloth so they could sit on the ground without getting dirty. Montgomery Gentry did all of their patriotic songs and got the crowd fired up in spite of the rain. Abby's favorite song was "My Town" and she sang along with everyone else when they played it. Announcers came on the loud speakers and announced that rain or shine the fireworks would go off as scheduled and everyone cheered. It wasn't long before the rain stopped leaving it more hot and muggy than before, air so heavy you could barely breathe.

At 9:30 the fireworks began going off. The fireworks display was choreographed with music from a local radio station and was indeed spectacular. Kristen and Abby were like little kids with their oohing and aahing over the fireworks. Every year the fireworks got more elaborate. Jerry and Jack looked around when people started screaming thinking they were screaming for the fireworks. Suddenly, everyone started getting up and began stampeding for the exits. Jack and Jerry jumped up and grabbed the girls, "Come on, I don't know what's going on, but let's get out of here." Jack shouted.

They started running as fast as they could. It was hard to run in the flip flops so they slipped them off and ran barefoot through the wet grass. The fireworks were continuing and throwing flashes of light over the stampeding crowds, but now no one was paying any attention to them. "Something must have happened, let's get Abby and Kristen out of here." Jerry yelled. They broke out of the crowd and instead of running with the crowd they ran down the hill toward Buffalo Bayou. The four of them ran along the bayou in the near darkness, slipping and sliding in the mud, and ran up the first stairway leading up to the street, bypassing much of the crowd. They made it back to the SUV in just a few minutes and Jack backed up the street to the first cross street and managed to get out of the area. The police scanner crackled and they heard that three people had been shot at the festival. Jack and Jerry looked at each other and shook their heads. *Not again. It had been a little over six weeks since the last shooting and I was beginning to think maybe it was over.* Jerry thought to himself.

They dropped the girls off and headed for the station. When they got to the station, they learned that someone with a high-powered rifle had shot and killed three people at the festival during the fireworks. There was so much noise from the fireworks, no one heard the shots nor saw the sniper. Other people around the victims noticed the bodies down and bleeding before they realized there was a sniper in the area. They had gotten up and ran and started the panicky stampede. The people, two men and one woman, had been sitting within fifty feet of each other beside the dandelion fountain on Allen Parkway. All three of them had been killed with one well placed shot from quite a distance. Once again the sniper had gotten away. So far, there were no reports of injuries other than the fatalities. No one knew if this was the same sniper or if there was more than one sniper. The guy or guys were damn clever.

Chapter Twelve

Monday, July 9, 2007

Jack's phone rang and when Abby started talking, he knew she was crying. "Abby, what's wrong?

"Mom went to the doctor today and he referred her to an oncologist. There's something not right with her white blood count."

"Oh Abby, I am so sorry. When does she see him?"

"She has an appointment on Wednesday. Dad is taking off work and he and I are going with her. Pete has to work."

"Is there anything I can do?" Jack asked.

"No, I just needed to talk to someone. I am so scared for her. What if it is cancer? I don't know what we will do."

"Don't start imagining the worse case scenario. Listen, you need to be strong for her. Don't let her know how scared you are. I'm sure she is scared to death also. Call me after you get home from the doctor's on Wednesday. You may not know anything that soon, but call me anyway. If you need me for anything, call me."

"I will. Thanks, Jack, I appreciate having you to lean on. I don't know what I would do without you."

Jack hung up the phone and called his mom with the news. "Oh Jack, I am so sorry. Keep me posted on what's going on. I hope Carol will call me so I can help her in anyway I can. I don't want to invade her privacy until she decides to tell me herself.

SHOTS

A lot of people who have cancer don't want to tell anyone because they don't want the pity. They are afraid that if they say they have cancer, you will treat them differently. I read somewhere that when someone tells their friends they have cancer, they give them the fear of cancer. Their friends can't think of them without thinking about cancer and people who have cancer don't want to be reminded of it with every conversation."

Karen had just hung up the phone when it rang again.

"Karen, it's Carol. I hope I'm not disturbing you."

"No, I'm not doing anything right now. What's up?" Karen closed her eyes, steeling herself for the news.

"I just came home from the doctor and I have to see an oncologist on Wednesday."

"Oh Carol, I am so sorry."

"I haven't been myself for about three weeks now. Well actually, I haven't been myself since Brandon was shot, but I thought it was just the shooting. I have been very tired and yet I can't seem to sleep when I go to bed. They did some blood work last week and I had to go to Dr. Jenkins today. Something's wrong with my white blood cell count. He referred me to an Oncologist at M.D. Anderson. Of course, when I told Abby, she went all to pieces. After what happened to Brandon, she has been so fragile and I hate to burden her with this. I am trying to be strong and positive for Ted and Abby and Pete, but I just had to talk to someone to get a handle on my fear. You know how we mothers are, we try to sugar coat everything to make it easier for the kids."

"Carol, I'm glad you called me. Please call me anytime, day or night, if you need to talk. What can I do for you?"

"Right now, all you can do is pray for me and pray for strength and courage for the family."

"I will and I will put you on the prayer chain at church."

"Thanks, that means a lot."

Karen thought a moment and said "Carol, I know you are going to be drained, at least emotionally when you get home from the doctor on Wednesday. Let me bring over my chicken enchilada casserole that evening for you. I know you like it and it is the least I can do."

"Thanks Karen. I really would appreciate that. I don't have much on an appetite these days, but I need to keep everything as normal as I can for the kids and Ted also. I'll see you Wednesday night. We'll talk then. Thank God for good friends."

Wednesday, July 11, 2007

Karen and Sam arrived at the Johnson's at 6:00 p.m. with the enchilada casserole and a large salad. Abby opened the door and hugged them both. She had been crying and she looked pale without any makeup. "Come on in, mom said you were bringing that delicious casserole." Abby took the casserole from Sam and Karen followed her into the kitchen with the salad.

"Abby, how are you doing?"

"I am so worried about mom. I just don't know what I would do without her."

"Your mom is going to be fine. You know what a fighter she is. Besides, you haven't heard anything yet, have you?"

"No, the doctor said maybe Friday. He ran some more tests today, did a chest x-ray and a cat scan, but couldn't tell us anything yet."

Just then Carol came into the kitchen. She was a little pale, but otherwise looked fine. She smiled and said "Boy, something sure smells good. Karen, thanks for bringing dinner.

Why don't you join us?" She mouthed the word *please* when Abby wasn't looking.

"Well, I did bring plenty, if you are sure it isn't an inconvenience."

Carol came over and hugged her. "Since when is having your best friend bring dinner and then eat with you an inconvenience. Abby, put two more place settings on the table. Karen and I will finish up in here."

When Abby had left the room, Carol whispered to Karen, "The doctor doesn't think it looks good. There was a huge spot on my lung. He will know more on Friday. I haven't told the kids and Ted yet, I just told them we wouldn't know anything until Friday. I wanted time to get used to the idea before I told them. Besides, maybe the doctor is wrong."

Karen hugged Carol and tried to give her strength. She didn't say anything, what could she say. Carol clung to Karen, taking what little comfort she could from her friend's embrace.

Conversation was a little forced at dinner, everyone tried to avoid the subject and talk about other things. Abby told Sam and Karen about the powdered sugar incident at the festival and about the shooting. Abby stressed how cool headed Jack and Jerry were, getting the girls out of the festival and back to the car. Pete told them about a heroic dog that had jumped on his masters' bed and woke them up when their house caught on fire. Everyone tried not to notice how little Carol ate.

After dinner, Karen helped Abby clear the table while Carol rested on the couch. "I'm so glad you came over tonight. Mom ate more with you here than she would have eaten if it were just us. She is very weak and so tired all the time."

"Abby, that's to be expected. Try to encourage her to eat frequently if she can't eat much at a time. She has to maintain her strength. She can't afford to lose any weight now."

They finished clearing the table and loading the dishwasher. Karen and Sam left shortly thereafter. "I'll call you on Friday." Carol called out as they left.

Abby walked them out to the car and hugged both of them, tears glistening in her eyes. "Thanks again for dinner and for staying to eat with us. We all needed the distraction. I hope this isn't as bad as it seems." Karen hugged Abby one last time before she got into the car.

On the way home, Karen filled Sam in on what Carol had said. "Karen, you are a good friend to her and she is going to need you in the coming weeks. I'll try to call Ted more in case he needs to talk. Knowing Ted, he will try to keep everything bottled up inside so he doesn't worry the kids. I know sometimes is it easier to voice your fears to someone outside the family than to those closest to you."

"It's hard for you men to open up to each other, that's where us women have an advantage over you. You're right, he will try to protect Pete and Abby and he will need someone to talk to. You are a good man, Sam. I love you." She said as she leaned over and kissed him. Karen pulled her cell phone out of her purse and called Jack to fill him in on the evening.

Chapter Thirteen

Friday, July 13, 2007

"Jack, can you come over to our house and bring your parents, we really need you."

Jack knew immediately that they had gotten bad news from the oncologist, he could hear the tears in Abby's voice. "I'll pick up mom and dad and we will be there as soon as we can."

Jack called his mom and told her what Abby had requested. "We will be ready when you drive up. I've been waiting to hear from Carol, but when I didn't, I was afraid the news wasn't good."

Carol met them at the door and embraced all of them. She hugged Karen the longest. Karen patted her on the back and held her close. They walked into the living room and sat down. Abby had made coffee and had put out a plate of Oreos. She poured coffee for everyone and with trembling hands handed each of them a cup. Pete sat on the end of the couch, his head hanging down and his hands clasped in front of him.

Jack could tell they had all been weeping. Ted's eyes were red-rimmed and he couldn't look at anyone. Carol picked up her cup and held it in both hands before taking a sip. "Dr. Peterson wasn't very encouraging. He thinks I may have lung cancer. I have to go in next week for an MRI. After the MRI, if it shows what he thinks it will, we will have to discuss treatment, surgery, whatever, depending on the stage of cancer."

"Oh Carol, I am so sorry. Is there anything we can do right now for you?"

"Just continue to pray for me, pray for all of us."

Abby burst into tears and ran into the kitchen. Jack got up and followed her. She was standing at the sink sobbing. He came up behind her and took her into his arms. She turned and laid her cheek on his chest. He held her tight while she cried not even noticing that her tears were soaking his shirt as his tears fell on her hair. He didn't have any words to comfort her. First Brandon, and now this, it was too much for her to bear, but he knew she was strong and somehow she would get through it. He promised himself he would be there for her as much as he could.

Pete came into the kitchen and Abby and Jack opened their arms and brought him into the circle. Jack thought about the song *Will The Circle Be Unbroken* and thought to himself, *this circle will be unbroken*. The three of them held each other and took what comfort they could from the closeness. "This really sucks." Pete said.

"You're right Pete, this really sucks." Jack replied as he held his two best friends close.

Chapter Fourteen

Wednesday, July 18, 2007

"Karen, I got the results back from the MRI. It's stage 3 lung cancer. The oncologist suggested removing part of the left lung and then either chemo or radiation. I'm going for a second opinion tomorrow, but it doesn't look good."

"Oh Carol, I'm so sorry, I don't know what to say. Do they think only one lung is involved?"

"They are pretty sure it is only the left lung at this time. I'm thankful for that. A person can live with one lung if they have to and I intend to live to see both Pete and Abby married and with kids. This damn old cancer isn't going to beat me out of being a grandmother."

"That's the right attitude. You have to be a fighter."

The second opinion was the same as the first and Carol began to prepare herself mentally for the surgery. She was putting her faith in the Lord and to a lesser degree in the surgeons. The surgery was scheduled for a week from Friday.

Friday, July 27, 2007

Ted, Pete and Abby were at the hospital early the day of the surgery. Carol was already a little dopey from the pre-surgery medication when they arrived, but she managed to smile at them. They held her close and prayed with her before the orderly came to take her into surgery. Jack and his mom came to the hospital about an hour later. They brought coffee and Danish and waited with Abby, Pete and Ted. Shortly after 2:00 p.m. the surgeon came out to talk to the family.

"Would you like to step in here," the surgeon asked as he held the door open to a small office off the waiting room.

"I would like for Jack and Karen to come in with us. They are as close as family." Abby declared.

The surgeon nodded ok, and held the door for all of them. Abby and Ted took the two chairs in front of the desk and the surgeon sat behind the desk. Pete, Jack and Karen stood by the door. "Carol came through the surgery just fine. Right now, it looks like the cancer was contained in the left lung."

"Oh thank God." Abby cried and grabbed her father's hand.

"We removed about one third of the left lung. The surrounding tissue looked clean. The initial biopsy didn't show any more cancer cells, but we will do some extensive testing to be sure. Carol will be in recovery and we will keep her heavily sedated for about six hours so she will be out of it until around 7:00 p.m. tonight. I would suggest you all go home and get some rest and come back this evening. We will keep a close eye on her over the next several years to monitor any changes in her white blood cells. We may have to do some radiation, we will know more when the biopsy comes back, but it looks good for now."

"Thank you, Doctor." Ted said with tears running down his face. When the doctor left, they all clung to each other in relief.

Abby turned to Jack and Karen. "Thank you so much for coming to the hospital today. The waiting was a little easier with you both here."

"Abby, why don't you and Pete go on home now. I want to stay here and be here when mom wakes up. And you know everyone from church is going to be calling so someone needs to be at home to keep them posted on her surgery. I'm not going to feel like calling everyone when I get home tonight. I know her friends are going to be worried about the results of the surgery and they shouldn't have to wait until tomorrow. Will you do that for me?" Ted asked.

Jack smiled at Ted. He saw right through the ruse. Ted wanted Abby to go home and get some rest and he knew she wouldn't do it if it was for her benefit. Probably none of them had slept last night, worrying about the surgery. "Come on, Abby, Pete, let's go have a bite of lunch and then we will give you a lift home. I will bring you back tonight when your mom is in a room. Maybe while you are gone, your dad will get a little rest while he is waiting for your mom to come out of the anesthesia." Jack could play the game as well as Ted could. He knew Abby would do anything for her dad. Ted winked at Jack when Abby and Pete agreed to it."

"I'm glad you didn't have to work today. It helped to have you both here."

Jack didn't tell Abby that he had asked for the day off so he could be with them at the hospital. There was so little that anyone could do at a time like this, this was the least he could do.

"Go on, honey. I'll call you when mom is awake." Ted hugged Pete and then Abby.

Abby and Pete reluctantly followed Jack and Karen out of the hospital. They stopped at Café Express for a late lunch. No one had much of an appetite, but at least Abby ate some baked potato soup and Pete had a grilled chicken sandwich. After lunch, Jack and his mom drove Abby and Pete to their house, "Thanks man, for the ride and for being there today." Pete said as he got out of the car and shook Jack's hand. Abby hugged first Jack and then Karen over the back seat and got out of the car.

Around seven o'clock, Abby called Jack. "Jack, mom is coming around. Pete and I are going to the hospital. Pete said to tell you that if you didn't want to come it was ok, he needs to have his car at the hospital, because he is on call."

"I don't mind. I'll meet you at the hospital. I imagine that your mom will still be in ICU so they will only let two of you in at a time for short periods of time. I'll see you there."

Abby was by herself in the waiting room when Jack walked into the hospital. She saw him right away and came over to him. "Thanks for coming. Pete and dad are in with her now. I saw her about an hour ago and her color is already better than it was. She is still a little out of it, but that's to be expected. She said they came to take her to the operating room in a white Cadillac convertible. I can't wait until she is over the anesthesia so I can kid her about that."

"I called mom and told her Carol made it through the surgery and that we were all up here. She is going to wait a couple of days and then she will be up to see your mom. She said to tell you to be sure and call her if there is anything at all she can do. With a surgery like this it is going to take a while for your mom to get back to normal." Since Abby wasn't stepping away from him, Jack continued to hold her in his arms and run his hands down her back. She signed and laid her head on his chest, resting against him and taking comfort from his strength.

"Thanks, I will call her if we need anything. As soon as Pete and dad come out, let's get dad to go down to the cafeteria and grab a bite. He hasn't eaten anything all day. I know that he is probably starved." Abby said as she stepped away from Jack.

SHOTS

"If he won't go to the cafeteria, I'll run out and grab him something and bring it back. I know how stubborn your dad can be."

Ted and Pete came out looking a little rumpled and very tired. Jack shook hands with both men and hugged Pete. "Are you guys hungry?" Jack asked. "I haven't had dinner yet. I know the food is lousy in the cafeteria so I can either go out and get us something or we can just grab a bite downstairs."

"Let's just go downstairs. I'm not very hungry. I'll tell the nurses where we will be. We can't go in and see Carol again for another hour and then only 2 of us for 10 minutes." Ted said.

"Abby said she was looking better."

"Her color is good and she is very upbeat. If anyone can beat cancer, mom can." Pete said.

Chapter Fifteen

Wednesday, August 8, 2007

Abby was sitting in the sun room reading when the phone rang. "Hello."

"Abby, John Marcus gave me tickets for tonight's Astros's game, twelve rows up from first base, even includes preferred parking. They are playing the Cubs. You want to go?" Jack asked.

Abby looked over at her mother resting on the couch. "Let me check with mom, hang on a minute. Mom, would you mind if I went to the Astros game tonight with Jack? I won't go if you would rather I didn't."

"Oh honey, please go. You have been hovering around me like a mother hen ever since I came home from the hospital. It will do you good to get out. Besides, your dad is here and I will be fine."

"OK Jack, You bet. Oswalt's pitching tonight and you know how I love him. What time are you going to pick me up?

"How about 5:30 p.m.?"

"Great, see you then."

Jack smiled as he put down the phone. He would never tell her how he had begged and pleaded with John for the tickets, hoping he could convince her to go. She had been cooped up in that house ever since her mother was diagnosed and this was the only thing he could come up with to get her out of the house. He knew the only place she had been was to drive her mom to the doctor for her follow-up appointments. He was glad to hear that Abby was beginning to sound like her old self. The five of them had loved baseball since they were kids. Their parents knew if they took one of the kids to a game they had to take them all. The parents really didn't mind because it was so much fun watching the kids and their enthusiasm for the game. For years, the four sets of parents had season tickets and took all the kids and went to the games as a group. Abby had been a tomboy all her life, maybe because her best friends were the four little boys. Once when Abby was about eight years old, a fly ball had been hit into their section and Abby had scrambled and beat the four boys to the ball. She was so proud of herself. She jumped up and danced on her seat and held the ball in her glove. She was so cute with her braids popping around her head and the camera man loved it. He had kept the camera on her for the longest time. Later, Jack's mom told him that the camera showed Abby dancing and in the background, the four little boys had their arms crossed on their chest and were pouting as they scowled up at her.

Jack pulled up in front of Abby's house and Abby came running out. She had on her Biggio jersey, an Astros sun visor and her baseball mitt. She looked like a teenager again. "Good thing you brought your mitt. These seats are right where a lot of foul balls are hit. I brought mine, also." Jack said motioning to the mitt in the back seat.

They pulled into the preferred parking lot and walked in on the Crawford side of Minute Maid Park. They stopped and got hot dogs, beer and French fries before they made their way to their seats. "Man, these are great seats. How did John get them?" Abby asked.

"His company has 6 season tickets and this is where they are. They gave John these two and he had to leave town and couldn't use them so he asked me if I wanted them. Jerry was busy and Pete had to work so I had to settle for you."

"Oh you jerk!" Abby said as she swatted him on the arm.

"Actually, I asked you first."

"I thought you had." Abby laughed.

The game was close, 4 to 3 in favor of the Astros at the bottom of the third. Abby looked up and said, "Oh look, the Kiss Cam is on us."

Jack laughed and kissed her. She was laughing as she grabbed him and kissed him back. He knew the second the kiss changed from fun to serious. She grew still in his arms and the kiss deepened. Surprised by the intensity of the kiss, he heard her breath catch in her throat and felt her heart hammering against his chest. Her arms tightened around his neck and her lips parted for him. He held her a few more seconds and then released her. She looked at him with a question in her big brown eyes. Jack decided to play it light. "That should make the 'censored' sign'," he laughed as he released her.

Abby relaxed and laughed also. At home games, the Astro's cameraman focuses on different couples in the audience and if it shows you, you are supposed to kiss each other. Sometimes people crawl all over each other or use a lot of tongue and a 'Censored' sign comes up. They had always got a kick out of different people's reactions.

The game went into extra innings, but the outcome was good because the Astros won 8 to 7. They followed the mob out of Minute Maid Park and made their way to their car. Traffic was always a bear trying to get out of the area and onto the highway. Abby and Jack were quiet and lost in thought on the drive home. When they pulled up in front of Abby's house, Abby turned to Jack, "Thanks for asking me. I'm sorry about the kiss. I don't know what got into me. I didn't expect that, I guess I just got carried away with the Kiss Cam and all."

Jack took hold of Abby's hand and gently pulled her to him. "I'm not sorry about the kiss. I didn't expect it, but I sure don't regret it. Good night, now." Jack said as he kissed Abby again. She didn't pull away and her arms slid around Jack's neck. Once again, he could feel her heart pounding through his shirt. He kissed her once more and then reached across her to open the door for her to get out. She smiled and got out of the car. He watched to make sure she got in the house safely and then drove away while he could still leave her. He sure as hell didn't regret it. He had felt the heat and the passion, and the kisses gave him hope for their future. *That was no brotherly kiss, that's for sure,* he thought.

Chapter Sixteen

Friday, August 10, 2007

Jack and Jerry had just arrived at the station when the call came in. There was another shooting, this time downtown on Smith Street. The area was populated with high rise office buildings and parking garages, right across the street from the old library. There were hundreds of places where a sniper could hide in the area. The officers at the station began collecting assault rifles, police wind breakers and Kevlar vests and running out to their vehicles. Everybody was desperate to catch this sniper. The shootings had gone on far too long and they weren't getting any breaks on it. More and more it looked like the sniper was military trained, the way he could get in and out of the area and not be seen or at least recognized, and the way he could pick his spots with easy exits, it just made sense. Knowing that though, didn't get them any closer to catching the guy. There didn't seem to be any rhyme or reason to where he would strike next. Traffic on Smith Street and Dallas Street was at a standstill. The officers had to park their vehicles several blocks away and make their way down Smith Street on foot. Pedestrians were running, trying to get inside buildings; drivers were abandoning their cars in the street and running for the shelter of the buildings. Most of these buildings were connected by an underground tunnel system. The sniper could easily hide his rifle in his vehicle and mingle with the crowd to make his getaway, coming back later for his rifle and his vehicle. Jack's radio crackled and he heard they had confirmed six dead, the number of injured was unknown. Jack and Jerry scanned people's faces and watched to see if they could spot anyone who looked suspicious, but all they saw were scared people.

Jerry walked toward a parking garage and motioned for Jack to follow him. People were trying to get out of the garage but the traffic on Smith Street was stopped, it was a log jam and quickly backed the traffic up all the way to the freeway. Office workers were coming back from lunch and trying to drive into the different parking garages. Jack hadn't heard any shots since he arrived and assumed the sniper was long gone by now, the same as the other shootings. When Jack and Jerry got to the first floor of the first parking garage, Jack could see the driver's side windows on four vehicles on Smith Street were shot out. He could make out three of the drivers slumped over the steering wheels; the fourth driver he couldn't see because of the glare on the windshield. There were several cars pulled up on the curbs and abandoned where drivers had run into the buildings. Traffic police were trying to direct traffic away from the intersection. The vehicles which had bullet holes were being gone over by the crime lab. Jack and Jerry walked up the ramp in the parking garage. They scrutinized every driver and checked out the backseats as they passed by their vehicles. Several of the drivers asked if it was safe to leave the garage. Jack told them it would be best to stay in the garage until they were sure the sniper was gone from the area. They walked all the way to the top of the six story parking garage. They didn't see anything or anyone suspicious so they made their way back down to the street level. Traffic police were still trying to get the traffic moving. They had called wreckers to tow away the damaged vehicles. Two of the lanes were cleared and traffic was slowly beginning to move out of the area. All of the officers and detectives were taking statements, the same as before. Again, no one had seen anything, no one knew where the gunshots came from nor how long they lasted. Jack looked up at the buildings and in nearly every window, saw people looking down at the street. One of the news helicopters was hovering right overhead and Jack could see the cameraman riding shotgun and hanging out the door, shooting footage for the evening news. He was strapped into his seat with some sort of leather harness which allowed him to hang halfway out of the helicopter as he was filming the action. Jack was sure the news stations would crucify them once again because they were no closer to catching the sniper than they were before. Every shooting made matters worse.

Chapter Seventeen

When they got back to the station, Jack called Abby and filled her in on the latest shooting. She didn't have long to talk because she had started teaching second grade at Kincaid, and she had to get back to the kids. She had such a way with kids that he knew she would be great at it. He smiled to himself when he thought back to his own second grade and how he had met Abby. "Abby before you hang up, do you want to grab a bite tonight and catch up on things? I haven't seen much of you since school started." He could hear the chatter of kids talking and giggling in the background.

"Sure, they have opened a new Italian restaurant on Memorial that I would like to try."

"I have a couple of things I have to do after work, but I will pick you up around 7:00 if that's ok."

"That will be fine. See you then."

Jack stopped and picked up a huge bunch of flowers for Abby's mom on his way to her house. Abby was wearing a cute little yellow sun dress and white sandals when she came to the door. Her long dark hair was tied back with a yellow ribbon. She looked like a ray of sunshine to Jack. "Are those for me?"

"Sorry, I should have brought two bunches, these are for your mom."

"I guess I know where I rate. Come on in, she will be thrilled. She is doing much better and has been getting out and about a little more this week. She even went to lunch with your mom one day."

"Jack, how good to see you, come here and give me a hug." Carol said.

Jack walked over to her and gave her a gentle hug mindful of her incision, kissed her on the cheek and handed her the flowers. "Here, I thought these might cheer you up, but you are looking great. Sure a lot better than the last time I saw you. How are you feeling?"

"About sixty percent. Everyday gets a little better. I am getting stronger and I've been out to dinner one night this week and lunch one day with your mom so I am improving. It seems to take so long to get my strength back. Everyone is still fussing over me and I'm starting to enjoy being the center of attention." She laughed.

"Mom, do you want me to put those flowers in water before we go?"

"Sure honey, and then bring them back in here so I can enjoy them.

Abby grabbed a crystal vase and quickly arranged the flowers in it. She carried it back in the living room and sat the vase on an end table close to her mother. Abby and Jack kissed her good bye and left a few minutes later. "Your mom really does look better and she seems so upbeat after all she has been through."

"Mom believes that attitude has a lot to do with healing and I agree. Turn right here, the restaurant is just down the block."

The restaurant wasn't very large, only about 30 tables and six booths along one wall. The tables were covered with red checked oilcloth and had the quintessential candles on wine bottles and the strolling violinist. The hostess showed them to a booth in the back. Abby slid in and was surprised when Jack slid in the same side instead of across from her. She could feel the warmth of his thigh pressing against her leg as he sat close to her. It sure wasn't an unpleasant feeling. As she opened her menu, Jack put his arm around her and leaned in close to look at her menu instead of opening his own. She could smell the spicy aftershave he always wore. Surprised, she turned to look at him. He cupped her chin in his hand and slowly kissed her, being careful to keep the kiss soft. When the kiss ended, she looked at him with wonder in her eyes. He smiled at her and his eyes crinkled in amusement. "I thought I would start with dessert first."

The waitress came over bringing a plate of herbs and a basket of bread. She sat the basket of bread between them, poured olive oil over the herbs and inquired about their drink preferences. They ordered glasses of Chianti. Jack took his arm down but didn't move away from Abby. He was encouraged when she didn't distance herself from him and he smiled to himself. He told her what few details he could about the downtown shooting and she filled him in on her teaching job as they broke bread and dipped it in the oil. Her eyes lit up as she told him about the kids in her class. She loved teaching second grade and she had him laughing over the stories she told. A little boy sitting behind one little girl cut her ponytail cut off at the scalp. Abby had sent the little devil to the principal's office and called the little girl's mother. The mother had thrown a fit and Abby had to listen to a tirade from her over Abby's lack of control in the classroom. Abby was patient and finally got the woman calmed down. Abby was such a loving and giving person, he knew she would make a terrific mother some day, hopefully the mother of his children.

The waitress brought their food and they talked and laughed like old times. As they were eating, the violinist came over singing "That's Amore." Jack looked at Abby and smiled. He thought the music was very appropriate. They finished their meal and Abby asked for a to go box. "There was so much food that there is no way I could eat it all. I'll take a to go box and mom can have it for lunch tomorrow. She loves Italian." Jack paid the bill and as they left the restaurant, Abby slipped her hand in his. "This was fun. For a while after Brandon died, I didn't think I would ever smile again or have fun. I still miss him, but it is getting better. Every one said it would take time and it did. I'll never forget him and I will always have a soft place in my heart for him."

They walked slowly back to the SUV. Jack opened the door for Abby. She laughed and said "Gee, this is like a real date."

"No, this is a real date, not like a real date," he said as he leaned in and kissed her again. He fastened her seatbelt and walked around to the driver's side. He started up the SUV and backed out of the parking space. Her lips felt bruised from the kiss and it seemed awfully warm in the car all of a sudden. Jack looked over at her and smiled. "Abby, I've loved you since the first time I saw you in the second grade. I didn't know it until the night that Brandon proposed to you. I was so jealous of him, it nearly cracked my face when I tried to congratulate you on your engagement. I never would have told you if Brandon hadn't been shot. I loved him like a brother and I loved you more. I would never have done anything to come between the two of you or your happiness. He's gone now, and I miss him like hell, but life is short and we never know what is going to happen next. If it's too soon for you to have feelings for me, I am willing to wait for as long as it takes. I just wanted you to know how I feel."

They were both deep in thought as Jack drove her home. He stopped in front of her house and got out and opened the door for her. She slipped easily into his arms as he helped her out of the car. He guided her over to the porch swing behind the wisteria and for a while, they necked like a couple of horny teenagers. Finally, he pulled away from her. "Abby, I better leave now. We have to work tomorrow and it's getting late. I meant it when I said I love you."

"Jack, I think I love you too, but it's so soon, I don't want to mistake loneliness for love."

"Take whatever time you need. I'll be here." He stood up and waited while she unlocked the door and stepped inside. He smiled as he drove back to his apartment reliving the evening in his mind. Things were definitely looking up for Abby and him.

Chapter Eighteen

Monday, August 20, 2007

Jack and Jerry had been on a routine call and were coming back from downtown on Memorial when they got the call. There were shots fired once again at the Loop 610 and Katy Freeway interchange. This was the first time the sniper had duplicated the location of the shootings. They could hear sirens screaming in the distance as they pulled their car to the side of Woodway. "I've got a feeling about this one, let's park here and check out the wooded area at the top of that elevation. It hasn't been that long since the first shots were reported." Jerry said as he whipped the car on to the side of the road and both men jumped out of the car, pulling their weapons as they did so.

At the same time, Jack and Jerry noticed the old red pickup truck parked off Woodway. The two detectives looked at each other, each thinking about the red pickup truck mentioned at the church shooting. They walked up over the rise off Woodway heading toward the freeway looking around in all directions. They saw the old man coming toward them right away. He was heading toward the old red pick up truck and he was carrying a semi-automatic sniper rifle. He was dressed in Army fatigues and was stumbling through the tall grass with a dazed look on his face. He had a full head of grey hair and looked to be in pretty good condition for his age. He was tall and thin and looked strong. Jack aimed his service revolver at the man and called out to him, "Sir, please put down the gun." As Jack was talking to the old man, Jerry was scanning the tree line to see if he could see anyone else in the vicinity.

The old man turned toward Jack and stared at him without comprehension. He looked at the rifle in his hand as though he didn't know how it got there. "Is this a gun?" he asked. "What am I doing with this gun?"

"I don't know sir, but please lay it on the ground." As Jack was talking to the man, Jerry, still scanning the tree line, was making his way around behind the old man with his revolver drawn also.

"Who are you?" The old man asked.

"Detective Oakley with the Houston Police Department. Put the gun down now."

The old man bent over slowly and laid the gun on the ground. Jerry ran up and grabbed the old man and patted him down to see if he had any other weapons on him. He pulled his arms behind him and cuffed him.

"Why are you feeling me?"

"I was making sure you didn't have any other weapons on you. Why don't you come with me and I will take you home."

"Where do I live? I forget. Do I know you? Are you my son Johnny?"

"I'm not your son. I am Detective Olson and this is Detective Oakley."

While this conversation was going on, Jack, put his gun back in the holster and pulled on rubber gloves. He carefully picked up the rifle. He could tell it had been fired recently because the barrel was warm and there was a distinct cordite smell to the rifle. "Jerry, I think we have our man. I don't know how he could shoot someone in his condition maybe he is carrying the gun for someone else." Jack said more quietly "I think he either has Alzheimers or dementia." Both Jack and Jerry had completed Crisis Intervention Training with the Houston Police Department. The classroom lectures, role-playing exercises and real life scenarios trained the detectives to recognize and to deal with people with drug problems or mental illness.

"Is there anyone with you?" Jerry asked.

"No, I am on patrol by myself. Buster was killed."

"Who is Buster?" Jerry inquired.

"Who?" said the old man.

"You just said Buster was killed, who is Buster?"

"I don't know any Buster. Who are you?"

It was obvious that they old man was confused. They guided him to their car and opened the back door for him. Jack opened the trunk and put the rifle in the trunk. Jerry was trying to get the man into the backseat of the car. "I'm not going anywhere with you, I don't know who you are. Help, Help me, these men are trying to kidnap me. Help me. Help me." The old man shouted and fought them with all his might. He was extremely strong for his age. Suddenly he just stopped fighting and was calm.

They were starting to draw quite a crowd of onlookers, mostly runners from Memorial Park. Jack and Jerry pulled out their badges. "It's ok, we are detectives with the Houston Police Department. We're taking this gentleman in for questioning. Do any of you know him?"

Several of the bystanders shook their head no.

Jack and Jerry were scanning the trees behind them trying to see if there was anyone there who might be the sniper or another sniper, but didn't see anyone. "Can you tell us your name?" Jack asked.

The old man started crying. "I don't know my name. I can't remember why I am here. I just want to go home."

"It's ok, get in the car and we will find out where you live and take you home."

The old man got in the backseat and Jack and Jerry closed the door to the backseat. They got in the car and started toward the station. "Hey wait a minute, this isn't the way to Willowbend." The old man yelled.

"What's on Willowbend?" Jack asked.

"That's where I live. 9814 Willowbend."

"And what is your name?"

"William Parker, Sergeant, United States Army, 11490007."

"Name, rank and serial number." Jack said quietly.

"What do you do in the army?" Jerry asked.

"I'm a sharpshooter. We were sent out today to get those Viet Congs." Jerry looked at Jack, both thinking the old man hadn't lost his skill as a sharpshooter if that was the truth.

"Who was sent out with you?"

"My buddies, but they are all dead now."

"How old are you Mr. Parker?"

"That's Sergeant Parker to you son."

"How old are you Sergeant Parker?"

"Who is Sergeant Parker? What's your name? Are you my son Johnny?"

Jack shook his head and pulled into the parking lot at the police station. "Let's take him inside and maybe we can find out where he lives and who is responsible for him."

Jerry helped the old man out of the car and Jack got the rifle out of the trunk of the car. They had radioed in that they had a suspect in the shootings and were bringing him into the station. The station was crowded when they brought the old man in and the other detectives and officers were snickering and laughing at Jack and Jerry, thinking they had made a mistake bringing this stumbling old man in as the sniper.

They took Mr. Parker into the conference room and asked him if he would like some coffee.

"Black with two sugars and make it snappy. I have to get back on patrol." Jerry stepped out to get the coffee and to call in the Chief.

The Chief walked in and introduced himself. "Are you Mr. Parker."

"That's Sergeant Parker, Sir." The old man replied, automatically responding to the Chief's uniform.

"Sergeant Parker, where were you this afternoon."

"On patrol, Sir."

The Chief raised his eyebrows at Jack. "Detectives Olson and Oakley said they apprehended you with a high powered rifle this afternoon around 2:00 p.m. Is that correct?"

"Who are you, do I know you?" The old man asked the Chief.

Jack motioned the Chief aside and whispered, "I think he either has Alzheimers or dementia. He seems to switch back and forth from thinking he is on patrol and not knowing where he is. He thinks Jerry is his son, Johnny. We picked him up over off Woodway by that grove of trees off I-10. He walked out of the trees carrying a high-powered rifle which had been fired recently. I left the rifle in the lab to see if they could match any of the bullets we found on the other shootings with it. There was an old red truck parked right by where we picked him up but we don't know if it belongs to him or not. He acted like he didn't know what a gun was one minute and the next he is giving us his name, rank and serial number. At one point, he told us he lived at 9814 Willowbend, but we don't know if that is correct or if he is remembering something from the past. "

The Chief walked back and sat down across from the man. "May I see your hands, please?" Mr. Parker held out his hands but Chief Bruin couldn't detect any gunpowder residue on them. "Could I see your driver's license?"

"Where is it?"

"Do you have a wallet with you?"

The old man reached in his pocket and handed the Chief a dirty handkerchief.

"Would you empty your pockets for me, please." The Chief asked.

The old man pulled out a hand full of change, a key ring with several keys on it one of which was the key to a Ford and a battered wallet and laid everything on the table.

The Chief flipped open the wallet to the man's driver's license. The name was William F. Parker. The date of birth was shown as March 13, 1936. The address read 9814 Willowbend. "Jack, you and Jerry get on over there and see who else lives there. This man probably doesn't live alone. If you can find a family member, bring them back with you. Mr. Parker, I need you to stay here for a while."

"Where am I? What have you done with my couch? Who are you?"

"Why don't you just sit here and drink your coffee and I will check in with you later." The Chief walked out and told one of the officers to keep an eye on Mr. Parker through the two way mirror. "Have Ben come in and check for gunpowder residue on his hands. I checked, but I didn't see anything. Maybe with the spray something will show up. Then we'll just leave him alone until we find out who he lives with."

Jack and Jerry pulled up to a large brick house with a wrap around porch on a quiet cul de sac. As they went up to the door, they saw a curtain twitch and someone peek out at them. They rang the doorbell and a woman called out, "Who is it?"

Jack and Jerry held up their badges to the glass door and told her their names. The door opened slowly and a very small white-haired lady peered up at them. "Have you found Bill? He let himself out this morning and he took his truck. He's not supposed to be out without me, because he suffers from Alzheimers. Is he ok?"

"Are you Bill's wife?" Jack asked.

"Yes. We will be married forty-seven years this September."

"We have Bill down at the station. He is ok, but he seems confused. What kind of truck does he have?

"It's an old red Ford truck. I don't drive it, I always take the car. He thinks I won't notice if he takes the truck. Is he in trouble? Is that why you are here?"

"Mrs. Parker, do you know if he owns any guns?" Jack asked.

"Oh my yes, he has a whole collection in the game room. We have to keep them locked up now because of his disease, but he likes to look at them. He was a sharpshooter in the war you know."

Jack raised his eyebrows at Jerry. "Could we see the guns please?" Jerry asked.

She led them down the hall to a room facing a pretty back yard. The walls were covered with glass gun cases containing several pistols and about 100 rifles, some of which were semi-automatics. The door to one of the cabinets stood slightly open and there were two empty hooks where another rifle had been hanging. A card identifying where and when the rifle had been purchased along with a description of the rifle itself was posted beside the empty space. Jack and Jerry were amazed at the variety and quantity of guns on display.

They looked at each other in awe. "Where did he get all these guns?"

She smiled and told them he had been a collector for years, ever since the war. "I think it was because he was an ace sharpshooter in the war. He used to go to gun shows all over the United States and bring back guns for his collection."

"Are these the keys to these cabinets?" Jack asked.

"Yes, I try to keep them hidden from Bill. Sometimes he thinks he is still in the war and he gets them out and pretends to shoot at things so I can't let him get the guns out anymore. He spends a lot of time in here just looking at them."

"How long has this rifle been missing?"

Mrs. Parker walked over and looked at the case and saw the empty slot. She pointed to the key ring with numerous keys hanging in the door lock "He must have found the keys again. This time I had them hid in a plastic bag in the bottom of a coffee can. I keep finding different places to hide them, but sometimes he finds them. Does he have that rifle with him now?"

"I don't know if it is that rifle. We have a rifle down at the station that he had with him when he was apprehended. Mrs. Parker, we are going to need you to come downtown with us. We found your husband wandering around the I-10 and 610 interchange where another shooting had taken place today. He had a rifle with him and we could tell it had been fired recently." Jack opened the glass door and removed the small card beside where the rifle had been and slipped it in an evidence bag.

Mrs. Parker started crying. "Oh no. I have tried so hard to keep him home and not let him get in trouble. Did he hurt someone? He has gotten so much worse since the beginning of the year. I just can't take care of him anymore. I keep thinking I should put him somewhere where he will be safe but he still has lucid moments every now and then, when he is my sweet old Bill. There's just the two of us now, we had a son Johnny, but he was killed in the service. Bill never got over it. He still looks for him everywhere. Poor, poor Bill. I'll get my keys and be right with you. Could I ride with you? I really don't like to drive downtown."

"We will take you downtown and bring you back with you are finished." Jack said. He smiled to himself. She reminded him of his grandmother. He watched as she dabbed her eyes with her handkerchief and slowly locked the door. He held out his arm to help her down the steps and into the car. Out at the curb, he opened the rear door of the car and helped her inside.

The three of them walked into the conference room where Mr. Parker was sitting with the Chief. The Chief caught their eye and shook his head. Mr. Parker looked up as his wife came into the room. "Mom, is that you?" he asked.

"No honey, it's Martha. I'm your wife, remember?"

"Martha? Do I know you?"

The Chief stood up and held out his hand to Mr. Parker. "Mr. Parker, why don't you go with Detective Oakley and he will take you someplace and let you lay down for a while. I know you are probably tired."

"I am tired. I want to lie down." Mr. Parker got up and followed Jack out of the room, not even glancing at his wife as he walked by her.

"Jack, put him in a holding cell till we can get this straightened out. Mrs. Parker, I'm Chief Bruin, please have a seat. Could I get you some coffee or tea?"

"Tea would be nice, if it's not too much trouble."

Jerry got up "I'll get you some and be right back."

The Chief held the chair for Mrs. Parker to sit down. "What is wrong with Mr. Parker, does he have Alzheimers?"

"Yes, he was diagnosed about four years ago, but he has gotten much worse since the first of the year. I have been keeping him at home with me, but I don't think I can do it anymore. He gets so confused and no matter where I hide his truck keys, he finds them every so often and gets away from me. Sometimes he still thinks he is in the war. I thought I had his gun case keys hidden so well this time that he couldn't find them, but he must have, because your detectives saw there was one gun missing and the keys were hanging in the gun case door."

"How many guns does he have?"

"Oh hundreds, he has collected guns ever since the war."

Jerry looked appalled. "Are there more guns that we saw in the game room?" That would explain why all of the shootings were with different rifles. He had his choice out of hundreds of guns.

"Oh my heavens yes. I didn't show you all of the ones in the garage."

"What did he do in the Army?" The Chief asked.

"He was a sharpshooter." She replied.

Jack came back into the room and handed her a mug of tea. "Mr. Parker fell asleep as soon as he put his head down. He will be ok for now. I've got Officer Franklin keeping an eye on him in case he wakes up. I have also called our police physician to examine him and to see about getting some medication for him."

The Chief turned back to her, "Mrs. Parker, we believe your husband has been shooting and killing people at different locations over the last few months. It started with a shooting at the St. Francis Episcopal Church on Piney Point last April and there have been several shootings since then. We are going to have to confiscate all the guns in your possession to find out if any of them were used in the shootings. Do we need to get a warrant, or will you give us permission to take them out of the house? We will give you a receipt for anything we take out of the house."

"Please, take them. If Bill isn't going to be there, I don't want them anywhere around. I don't really like guns. When I go home I will show you where he keeps the ammunition and the gunpowder as well as the rest of the guns. What's going to happen now?"

"We are going to put Bill in protective custody for his own safety as well as the safety of others. The District Attorney will probably have him examined by our psychiatrist and if he deems him to be incompetent, we will have to put Bill in a Neuropsychiatric Center. I don't believe he will be able to stand trial in his condition. I'm sorry. We believe he is the 'Houston Sniper' as the papers have been calling him. We will run ballistics on the rifles to see if any of them were used in the shootings." The chief said.

"Had you heard about the shootings this year, Mrs. Parker?" Jack asked.

"A little bit, I don't watch the news and I don't take the newspaper. Too much bad news and I just don't want to hear it. I heard the ladies talking about some shootings once at church, but I didn't pay any attention. I never dreamed it might be Bill." Mrs. Parker looked stricken and her eyes pooled with unshed tears. "I'm so sorry. I thought I could handle him. He started slipping out while I was taking naps. I never dreamed he was taking his guns and shooting people. The poor families, I am so sorry. Will I be able to visit him wherever you put him?"

"I'm sure you will." The chief turned to Jerry. "You and Jack drive Mrs. Parker home and stay with her. I am going to get a couple of officers to get the panel truck and come over and pick up the guns and ammunition. You will need to inventory everything they take out of the house. Grab a laptop and set up an inventory right on the laptop. That will be faster. Have the truck towed in and tested for fingerprints to see if anyone else was in the truck besides Mr. Parker." The chief handed Jack the key ring he had taken from Mr. Parker.

Then to Mrs. Parker, "Thanks for coming in and thanks for letting us take the guns and ammunition without a search warrant. The quicker we can get all this nailed down, the better it will be for Bill and for all of us. Don't worry about your husband, he's safe now, he can't hurt himself or anyone else now."

After Mrs. Parker left, Max Shafer handed the Chief a cup of coffee. "Chief, what I don't understand is how someone with Alzheimer's could plan and carry out the shootings the way Mr. Parker did."

"Sniper training is so intense and exact that once a person has it, their actions when they are on patrol become automatic. I would imagine that when Mr. Parker picked up a rifle, his Army training just took over and it was so routine for him to conceal himself, shoot fast and deadly, pick up his casings and carefully disappear from the area that he didn't even have to think about it. It's just pure damn luck that Jack and Jerry saw that old truck and stopped to investigate or it might have been a long time before we caught him. Then again, maybe his Alzheimer's is getting so bad, he wouldn't have been able to do it much longer."

"Well, I am sure glad it's over."

"Me too, Max. Me too. You know I have a mother in an Alzheimer's unit up by Austin. She thinks she is running a boarding house and when we go to visit her, she doesn't know us, but she makes people get out of their beds and sit on the floor so we can have a room in her hotel. She orders the nurses and nurses' aids around and tells everyone what to fix for dinner. She plans all these elaborate dinners and writes out grocery lists. This fantasy sometimes goes on for weeks at a time. The nurses just humor her and go along behind her putting people back in their beds. That takes a lot of planning and then she doesn't even remember my name or recognize me most of the time. It's a strange disease."

Chapter Nineteen

Jack and Jerry drove Mrs. Parker home. She was crying softly in the back seat and Jack kept glancing at her in the rearview mirror. Jerry opened the door and helped Mrs. Parker up the stairs. She walked back into the game room and took the keys from the case and began opening the cases. Jerry cleared a spot on the desk and sat the laptop down. There were all kinds of gun cleaning supplies sitting around the perimeter of the desk. He noticed one small cabinet filled with shooting awards and pictures of a young man being awarded the Purple Heart by President Kennedy, and pictures of a young Bill Parker with various Army officers receiving other awards. There was a picture of an older Bill Parker with a young marine."

Mrs. Parker noticed him looking at the picture. "That's our son, Johnny on his first leave out of boot camp. Bill was so proud of him when he joined the Marines."

"Bill must have been a very good sharpshooter judging by all these awards." Jerry said.

"He was the best they ever had. Officers that Bill had served under used to come by from time to time and they all told me that. That picture there is my Bill receiving the Purple Heart from President Kennedy. You know a lot of people didn't believe in the war, but Bill was a true patriot. He loved his country and he was proud to serve. When Johnny volunteered for the Marine Corp, Bill was so proud. Johnny had only served two years when he was killed in Afghanistan. Bill never got over that and sometimes he still talks to him and walks through the house looking for him. It has gotten worse since the Alzheimers was diagnosed."

Jerry examined the photos a little longer and felt sorry that Bill Parker had to end his life in disgrace after serving his country so valiantly for so many years.

"Would you like to see the guns in the garage now?" Mrs. Parker asked.

They followed her through the house, and out the back door to the detached two car garage. "I always leave my car out and Bill puts his truck over there on that side of the garage. It's hard for me to pull my car in the garage. That's why I don't miss his truck when it's gone. This side of the garage is where he built all the cabinets for the rest of his guns and ammunition."

As Mrs. Parker opened the door, Jack and Jerry were amazed at the number of guns on display. There was row after row of all different types of handguns and rifles. Like the display cases inside, each gun had a small neatly printed label telling the make, model and the year it was manufactured. In many instances, Mr. Parker had noted who he bought the gun from and the date it was purchased. These little labels would make inventorying the guns much easier. Jack and Jerry noticed three blank places where rifles had been. The descriptive labels were in place, but the rifles were gone. "Mrs. Parker, do you know where these guns could be?" Jerry asked, pointing to the empty spaces in the display case.

"No, sometimes Bill would switch a gun from out here to a display case in the family room, but he never left the label on the empty space. Course, with the way he is now, I guess it's possible he could have forgotten." Mrs. Parker opened a large chest in the corner. "This is where he kept the ammunition."

There were clips and boxes of ammunition for every caliber of gun and rifle imaginable. At first glance, there looked to be at least 500 boxes of ammunition. There were enough guns and ammunition to outfit a small Army. Jack and Jerry looked at each other and shook their heads. "It's a wonder some drugged up junkie hasn't broken into the house or garage and stolen all these guns." Jack said.

"Well, I better get inside and start on that inventory before they come to pick the guns and ammunition up." Jerry said. "Jack, how about you reading me the labels from the guns and I will start the inventory and you can attach the matching label to each gun and start stacking the guns ready to be picked up when the panel truck gets here. I guess I better call the Chief and ask him where he wants the truck to take them, there isn't room in the evidence room at the station for all of these guns. We will probably have to test fire the rifles to find out if any of them are the rifles used in the other shootings. This is going to take forever."

Jack and Jerry worked for about two hours before the panel truck showed up. Two officers from the station came inside and began carrying out the guns and stacking them in the back of the truck. As Jerry finished putting the descriptions in the inventory, Jack attached the label to the corresponding gun and stacked it by the front door. They worked steady for several hours. Finally Mrs. Parker asked them if she could fix them a bite to eat. They didn't want her to have to fix them dinner, but she insisted. "It will give me something to do." She told them.

They worked for another half hour and she called them into the dining room. The table was set with her fine china and cloth napkins. She showed them a small bathroom down the hall from the dining room where they could wash up before dinner. The two officers and Jack and Jerry sat down and bowed their heads as Mrs. Parker said grace. She passed Jack a small bowl of mashed potatoes. It took Jack a minute to realize the potatoes were for all of them and not just his serving. There were also canned green beans and five fried chicken drumsticks. Jack was having a hard time keeping a straight face, he looked at Jerry and winked. He hadn't got by on this small amount of food since he was a kid. After they had eaten, Mrs. Parker brought out small dishes of canned peaches for dessert and refilled their coffee cups. They finished the meager meal and by the time they got all the guns and ammunition inventoried, it was close to 3:00 a.m. In all, Mr. Parker's collection included 57 pistols, 217 rifles and over 500 boxes of different types of ammunition. Mrs. Parker had fallen asleep on the couch.

Jack walked over and gently touched her arm. She awoke with a start. "Oh my goodness, I'm sorry I must have fallen asleep. What time is it?" She asked.

"It's nearly 3:00 a.m. We finished inventorying and loading the guns and ammunition and we are leaving now. Sorry it took so long. We will send you a copy of the inventory of the items we took with us after we get back to the station and print it out. Here's my card and Jerry's card in case you have any questions or we can help you with anything." Jack held out his hand and helped her off the couch.

Mrs. Parker followed them to the door and turned on the porch light for them. She stood and watched them go out to their car and she slowly closed and locked the door. She walked back to the couch and sat down with the tears streaming down her face. Mrs. Parker supposed she would have to sell the house and move into a small apartment close to wherever they put Bill. Since Bill had gotten so bad, she had known the house was too big for her to take care of and that she needed to move to something smaller. Poor Bill and those poor families of the people he had shot. She still couldn't believe it. She had no idea that he was capable of such a thing. She knew he wasn't himself when he did it but that didn't make it any easier for the families. And all those guns, maybe they could be sold and the proceeds given to the victims' families. She made a mental note to call that nice young detective and ask him about that.

Chapter Twenty

Jack and Jerry stopped by the station long enough to drop off the laptop and then they headed out. The Chief was still in his office and motioned them in. "We got some prints out of the truck that didn't belong to Mr. Parker. We are running them through CODIS now. We didn't find any residue on Mr. Parker's hands, but maybe he wore gloves and disposed of them before you found him. I'm getting ready to head out. You guys look like you are dead on your feet. Go on home, get some rest and you can polish the inventory and give it to me tomorrow."

"Man, I'm beat. I think I could sleep for a week." Jack said to Jerry as he was getting into his car.

"I feel sorry for Mr. and Mrs. Parker, but I am so relieved we finally got him. It was pure damn luck that we happened to be there when he was coming back to his truck. If we hadn't got him then, who knows how many more might have died at his hand. He is still a hell of a sharp shooter, imagine what he was like in his prime." Jerry replied. "Well, it's going to be a short night. We will have to come in first thing tomorrow and catch up on the paperwork on Mr. Parker. See you then."

Jack parked his car in his designated spot and made his way into his apartment. He dropped his clothes by the bed and fell across the bed not bothering to even get under the spread. He awoke the next day with the sun streaming in the windows. His mouth felt fuzzy, his eyes gritty from lack of sleep. He looked at his watch and saw it was nearly 11:00 a.m. He would have turned over and gone back to sleep but then he remembered the mountain of paperwork to be done with regard to the shootings so he dragged himself out of bed and into the shower. He set the coffee to brewing as he shaved and dressed. Feeling half-way human, he grabbed a cup of coffee and called Abby.

His heart lightened when she answered the phone. "Abby, we got the sniper yesterday."

"I know. I just saw on the news where you had a suspect in custody."

Jack reached over and flipped on the small TV on the kitchen counter. Channel 2 was just finishing up the noon broadcast. "Shoot I missed it. What did they say?"

"They said the Houston police arrested a suspect in the 'Houston Sniper' case and that nearly 300 guns and 500 boxes of ammunition were seized from his house. The Chief of Police read a statement saying a 71 year old man suffering with Alzheimers was apprehended with a high powered rifle in the area of the latest shooting yesterday afternoon. He mentioned you and Jerry by name saying the apprehension was due to the quick thinking of Detectives Oakley and Olson."

"Abby, it was pure damn luck. Jerry and I saw an old red truck parked on Woodway and we were just checking out that wooded hill at 610 and 10 when this old guy comes walking out of the woods towards the truck carrying a rifle. He didn't know who he was nor where he was. He didn't even realize that he was carrying the rifle. We took him in and finally the Chief got him to give him his wallet. We found out who he was and where he lived and went over there. His wife didn't know where he was. She admitted he had Alzheimers and he had slipped out of the house without her knowing. She showed us case after case of guns and one of the cases was unlocked and a rifle was missing out of it. That was the gun he had with him and it had been fired recently. She went down to the station with us and he didn't even know her. He thought it was his mother. His wife didn't know anything about the shootings. She doesn't watch the news nor take a newspaper because it is too depressing. She is a sweet old thing and she let us take all the guns and ammunition out of the house. We were there until nearly three a.m. this morning. I felt so sorry for her."

"How awful for her. You and Jerry must be exhausted."

"I am, we went home around 4:00 and I just got up. The old guy thought he was still in the army. He was a sharpshooter who won all kinds of awards for his shooting. He was even awarded the Purple Heart by President Kennedy. I need to go now, I've got to get into the station and help Jerry finish up the paper work. I will talk to you later."

Abby put the phone down and told her mother what Jack had said. "I'm so glad they finally caught this guy. I know it doesn't help you with losing Brandon, but at least you know that it wasn't done on purpose. Just a confused old man who didn't know what he was doing. Maybe you can start to put this behind you now, honey and get on with your life."

"Mom, would you think I was awful if I told you I think I am falling in love with Jack. I can't believe it's happening so soon after I lost Brandon."

"Honey, I've seen that coming for a while. Jack has always been devoted to you, but you never noticed because of Brandon. I see the way he watches you and takes care of you. He's a good man. I think he has always loved you."

"Remember the night he took me to the Astros game, the kiss cam focused on us and when I kissed him, something happened. The kiss turned into a lot more than just a casual kiss. I think he was as surprised by it as I was."

"What did Jack say about it?"

"Oh he laughed it off, but I could see by his eyes he felt the same thing I did. Later I tried to apologize for the kiss and he told me he wasn't sorry. I've been thinking about him a lot more lately. But what if I'm wrong and he is just being nice to me because of what happened to Brandon? What if we are just lonely and looking for someone to ease the pain. Who knows, maybe we are just taking comfort from each other because we both miss Brandon so much."

"Abby, just go along like you have been and if it develops into something more than friendship, you will know when the time is right. Jack is smart enough not to rush you into anything, He always was the most level-headed of all you kids."

Chapter Twenty-One

Monday, August 27, 2007

A few days later, Jerry motioned Jack over when he saw him come into the station. "Guess what, I asked Kristen to marry me and she said yes."

"You dog, you, that's great. When's the big day?"

"Sometime next spring. We haven't decided an exact date yet. I want you to be my best man. I know Kristen is going to ask Abby to be the maid of honor."

"You know I will be honored to be your best man." Jack said as he hugged Jerry. "I always thought I would beat you getting married as slow as you move."

"Sometimes slow is good!" Jerry said as he winked at Jack.

Abby was surprised to see Kristen pull up in her driveway. "Kristen, what are you doing here? I thought you and Jerry were attached at the hip, I never see you without him anymore." Abby held the door open for her friend.

"I was just in the neighborhood and thought I would drop by and see your mom."

"Come on in, would you like a coke?"

"Sure, notice anything different about me?"

"Other than you are smiling like an idiot? No, not really. What's up?"

"You sure you don't notice anything different?" Kristen said as she waived her left hand in front of Abby's face.

"Oh my God, is that an engagement ring on your finger? It's gorgeous. When did that happen?"

"Last night at Vargos. Jerry wanted to go somewhere special and I didn't know why. When they brought our salads, there were three plates with those silver covers on them. They uncovered each of our salads and then they sat the third plate on the table and when they took the cover off, there was the engagement ring on a little white satin pillow. Then Jerry got down on one knee right in front of everyone and asked me to marry him. Everyone cheered when I said yes. It was so romantic."

Abby hugged her friend. "I am so happy for you. Jerry's a great guy and I know how much he loves you. When's the big day?"

"We are thinking sometime in the spring. Of course, I want you to be my maid of honor. Jack is going to be the best man."

"Here's your coke. Let's go show your ring to mom. She will be as thrilled as I am."

"What are you two girls giggling and carrying on about?" Carol said as she walked into the kitchen.

"Look here," Abby said waiving Kristen's hand in front of her mother's face. "Kristen and Jerry are engaged."

"Oh Kristen, your ring is beautiful. I am so happy for you and Jerry. When did that happen?"

Kristen repeated the Vargo story and about asking Abby to be the maid of honor. Kristen went on to tell them that they were going to be married at St. Cecilia's Catholic Church and that they planned on renting an apartment until they could afford a house.

Chapter Twenty-Two

Friday, September 14, 2007

Jack walked into the station and it looked like all hell was breaking loose. He grabbed one of the officers rushing by. "Hey man, what's happening?"

"There was another shooting, this time in the Greenspoint area. We are all heading up there. The guy will probably be gone by the time we get there. Talk to the Chief, I've got to go."

Jack ran into the Chief's office. The Chief was on the phone and motioned Jack into a chair. "Christ, that's all we need. I'll get right on it." The Chief said as he hung up the phone. "Jack, I'm glad you are here, we have another sniper attack up by Greenspoint Mall. Grab Jerry and get geared up and get up there. The call came in about six minutes ago. Same M.O. as before. He killed some people on Beltway 8. Don't know how many yet. I thought we had the bastard. This must be a copy cat shooting."

Jack grabbed two of the riot guns and two Kevlar vests as he walked by the supply officer. He saw Jerry come into the station and he motioned him over. "We have sniper fire reported up on Beltway 8 by Greenspoint Mall. You want to drive or shall I?" Jack asked as he slipped into the bulletproof vest.

"I will. Is this a copycat shooting? Mr. Parker's still in custody."

"I don't know. Let's get up there." The two men joined the crush of officers and detectives exiting the building. As they pulled out of the lot, Jack told Jerry that he should try to get up there by back roads, because he heard one of the guys saying all the freeways were jammed up all around the area. If it was like before, they knew the shooter would be long gone before they could make their way into position.

Jerry took Greens Road and they could see Route 45 and the Beltway both had traffic backed up for miles. Jack could see at least nine cars on the Beltway with the driver's side window shot out. It looked like the shooter had been shooting from the north side of Beltway 8. There were several hotels and office buildings with parking garages that faced the Beltway. Jerry parked his truck behind one of the hotels and they ran toward the feeder road. He and Jack listened but didn't hear any shots. Not surprising since it was 20 minutes since the calls came in regarding the sniper fire. Jerry grabbed his binoculars and scanned the rooftops and balconies of the hotels to see if he could spot the shooter. There were people on many of the balconies staring and pointing at the mess on the freeways. Jack couldn't see anyone with a rifle on the roof of the parking garage nor at several levels in the garage. *Shooter's probably not there*, he thought to himself. He would want to be in a secure place and he would want to be alone to do the shooting.

Jack looked up and saw the news helicopters circling overhead. He could see camera men filming the area through the windows of the helicopters. Damn, this was going to be another media circus, the TV stations would crucify them over this. Everybody was so sure that Mr. Parker was the shooter and when he was arrested, they thought they could put this behind them. The police had not yet been able to check the ballistics on all the guns with all the shootings. There were just too many rifles. The rifle that Mr. Parker had with him the day he was arrested matched the shootings for the day he was caught, but not for any of the other shootings. Now it looked like there was another sniper. If they were working together, Mr. Parker was in no condition to identify the other sniper.

Jerry could see the wreckers were lining up to remove the wrecked cars. Several of the vehicles had spun out of control and hit other vehicles. There were twelve ambulances that he could see, five of which were stopped by vehicles and the EMTs were treating injured parties. Jack saw them help one woman up on a stretcher and he could see blood on her head. They put her in the back of the ambulance and one of the EMTs got in with her, while the other one went back to the vehicle she was in and came back carrying a small child. It looked like her car had been hit by a car that went out of control. From that angle, Jack couldn't see any bullet holes in the woman's car windows.

Traffic police were working their way through the cars, directing some drivers to drive down the embankment and guiding others around the wrecked vehicles trying to clear the area as best they could. A road block had been set up in both directions on the Beltway and on Interstate 45 and traffic was being diverted onto the feeder roads. This would take hours to clear up. Jack knew they would get all the vehicles that could be moved out of the way and the crashed vehicles which weren't shot would be towed off to impound lots. Then the crime scene would come in and measure for trajectory and they would try to figure out where the sniper or snipers had been to make the shots. Officers and detectives would comb the area for shell casings and anything the sniper might have left behind.

"Let's go talk to some of these drivers around the vehicles whose windows have been shot out. We probably aren't going to learn anything because this shooting is just like all the others." Jerry said as he started climbing the embankment toward the Freeway.

Jack walked up to a BMW with a blond middle aged woman behind the wheel. She was resting her face on her arms leaning on the steering wheel. She looked up at him with tears streaming down her face as he tapped on the window. He showed her his badge and she rolled down the window. "Are you ok, ma'am?"

She shook her head no and continued sobbing. Jack couldn't see any injuries on her but she was unable to tell him what was wrong. Finally, she blurted out, "That's my daughter up there in the red Volkswagen. The policeman told me I had to stay back here. She's eight and a half months pregnant and I am so worried about her.

"Come with me, ma'am. I'll take you to her." Jack helped the woman out of the car and started toward the red Volkswagen. One of the traffic officers yelled for them to stay back. Jack showed his detective badge and explained the situation.

"Go ahead."

As they walked up to the car, Jack heard the woman screaming. "Oh my God, the baby is coming, somebody help me. Help me."

Jack yelled for the EMT "Over here, over here right now. We have a woman in labor." He opened the door to the car and gently turned the woman so she was sitting facing him. He could see her water broke and just as he turned her, she was hit with another contraction. Two EMTs came running up. Jack stepped back and let them do their job. The woman's mother had walked around to the passenger side of the car and was supporting her daughter's back from behind and trying to get her to calm down.

One EMT crouched before the woman and slid her blood soaked maternity pants and underwear off. "What's your name?" He asked.

"Kelly."

"Ok, Kelly, I'm Chuck. You need to stay as calm as you can. Everything is going to be all right. Your mom is behind you and I've delivered babies before and I'm going to get you through this. I can see your water has broken. How far apart are the contractions?"

"Real close, about two or three minutes apart."

"Take deep breaths. Hold on to Bill's hand and when the next contraction comes, I want you to push."

Just then another contraction hit and the woman screamed and nearly broke Bill's hand with her squeeze.

"That's good Kelly. Push. Breathe now, breathe."

People from the surrounding cars were trying to see what was going on. Jack grabbed a traffic officer and had him start moving what cars he could away from the Volkswagen and to keep people back. He grabbed a blanket from the gurney and held it up as a privacy shield around the woman.

Kelly screamed again. "Push, push, you are doing fine."

The next contraction came. "Ok, I can see the crown. We are nearly there. Push. Push. Breathe now. You are doing great." Bill reached behind him and took a cloth from the medic bag and gently wiped Kelly's forehead.

"Kelly, on the next contraction, I want you to push as hard as you can. Everything will be ok. Here we go, push, that's a good girl."

A few minutes later, her baby boy was born. Bill took the baby from Chuck and Chuck cut the umbilical cord. Bill wrapped the baby in a blanket and stood back. "OK, Kelly, you did great. You have a beautiful baby boy. Now let's get you on this gurney and get you and the baby to the hospital to be checked out, everything is going to be just fine."

Jack was grinning like a fool. "That was an absolute miracle." He hugged Kelly's mom as she came around the car. "Do you want to ride to the hospital with Kelly?"

"What about our cars?"

"Give me your address and I will see that they are towed to your house."

The woman quickly scribbled her name and address in Jack's notebook. She hugged him one more time and said "Thank you so much. I'll never forget this."

Jack grinned and said "Oh boy, neither will I!" Then to the EMT's "What hospital are you taking her?"

"Northwest Memorial." Chuck shouted as he put Kelly and the baby in the ambulance and turned to help her mother inside.

Just then Jerry walked up. "Jerry, guess what?"

"I wondered where you were. They are starting to get the traffic moving out of here now. What's going on?"

"A woman just went into labor and had a baby right here. Man, that was something. She was in this Volkswagen and it was a baby boy. I guess the stress of the shooting brought on labor or something. I can't believe it."

"Man. I can't believe I missed it. Did you have to deliver it?"

"No, the EMTs came over right after her water broke."

"Hey, I need a couple of wreckers over here." Jack shouted to the wreckers lined up to tow vehicles away. "These two vehicles need to be towed to 14470 Spring Shadow Glen and left in the driveway, here's my card, send the bill to me. Thanks. Jerry, anything new on the shooter?

"No, it is like all the others. Fast shoot and fast get away. The trajectory seems to come from the roof of that parking garage. Some of the other detectives are checking it out now. I believe there are five dead and several injured. They are taking the injured to Northwest Memorial. Some of the injuries are from vehicle incidences."

"Well, we better get back to the station and help out with the paperwork on this latest shooting. You know it will be a mess. I thought we were finished with all of this."

When Jack and Jerry got back to the station, it was once again a mad house. People were yelling and shouting across the room at each other and phones were wringing off the wall. The Chief motioned Jack and Jerry into his office. "We caught a break on this shooting. One of the shell casings rolled under some leaf debris on the roof and the metal detector picked up on it. Ballistics have the casing now. We got one smudged fingerprint off it and we are running it through CODIS. It is a match to one of the prints found in Mr. Parker's truck, but so far not to anyone in CODIS. Also, one of the witnesses saw a new black Honda truck leaving that garage in a big hurry. He didn't get the license plate, but he caught a glimpse of a young white man driving it. That's more than we got on the other shootings. Can you two start typing up the notes taken at the scene and we will see if anything else comes together from this."

Jack and Jerry sat at their desks and started imputing the witness statements taken at the scene. A couple of hours later, the Chief came back and asked for what they had done. He told them there would be another press conference at 4:30 p.m. so the news people could get it on the news. Jack decided to take a break and call Abby.

"Abby, I just wanted to let you know there has been another freeway shooting. This time it was on the Beltway by Greenway Plaza. Turn on the news as we had a news conference just a few minutes ago. You know what else? In the middle of all of that, a woman went into labor and had a baby right there on the freeway. I thought I was going to have to deliver it, but there were some EMTs already on the scene and they delivered a little boy. Mom and baby seemed to be doing fine. Man, that was something."

"Oh my gosh. How exciting about the baby. I don't understand about the shooting though. I thought Mr. Parker was responsible for all the shootings and he's still in custody, isn't he?"

"Yes, he's still in custody. We will have to look at everything again now. We know the rifle that Mr. Parker had with him when he was picked up was the rifle used in that particular shooting, but it wasn't used in any of the other shootings. We thought maybe he wore gloves when he did the shooting because he didn't have any gunshot residue on his hands when he was arrested and that would fit with not finding any fingerprints from any of the shootings."

"I thought we were through with all of this and now it's starting back up again." Abby saw her mother come in the kitchen. "Mom, quick turn on the TV. There has been another freeway shooting."

Jack snagged two cokes from the vending machine and carried one back to Jerry. "I've been thinking about those three missing rifles from Mr. Parker's garage. Suppose someone was taking advantage of Mr. Parker's condition and it really wasn't him doing all those shootings. Do you know where those notes are from when we picked up Mr. Parker?"

Jerry flipped through the box of files from the shootings. "Here's a copy of the Parker interview." He said and handed the pages to Jack.

"Here it is, he said he was on patrol with Buster, but Buster got killed. Maybe Buster didn't get killed and that is who the real shooter is. I think we need to go out and talk to Mrs. Parker again. Maybe she knows a Buster."

Jack ran a copy of the interview to take with them and put the original back into the file. They stopped by the Chief's office and told him what they were thinking. "Check it out. Maybe she does know something and doesn't even realize. Call me if you get anything."

Chapter Twenty-Three

Mrs. Parker was sitting in the porch swing on her big white porch when Jack and Jerry drove up. She smiled when she recognized them. "Hello again. How nice of you boys to stop by. Would you like some iced tea? I just made it."

"No, thank you ma'am. We just came by to visit with you." Jack said as he and Jerry walked up on the porch. Jack sat beside Mrs. Parker on the old fashioned porch swing and Jerry perched on the railing facing them. "Mrs. Parker, do you remember Mr. Parker talking about a 'Buster'?" Jack asked.

"Yes, Buster was someone who was in the Army with him. I gathered that Bill thought a lot of him."

"You don't know of anyone else named Buster that he might have known more recently?"

"Not that I can think of. Oh, wait a minute. Beau Hendrix is a young man who lives in the neighborhood. He mows our lawn for us. He has been coming over for years to visit with Bill and Bill was teaching him to shoot out at that range on Westheimer. Then after Bill was diagnosed with Alzheimers, sometimes Bill would get confused and call him Buster and sometimes he even called him Johnny, you know, he thought he was our son, Johnny. I thought Bill was being funny when he called him Buster. Bill would say things like 'Listen here Buster, that rifle is older than you are.' You know, things like that."

"Do you remember the last time that Bill took Beau to the range?" Jack asked.

"It was probably a couple of months ago. Beau got a new truck and he came over to take Bill for a ride. I know they took rifles with them and Beau told me not to worry because he was taking him out to the range and he would watch out for him. Bill loved going to the range with Beau. Beau is such a nice young man. Most young men couldn't be bothered with an old man with Alzheimers. Bill always seemed more coherent when he had a gun in his hands. Though sometimes, they would come back from the range and Bill would forget that they had even been there. He would say things like 'I wonder when Johnny is coming home to take me shooting.' and one time when they had been out shooting, he said 'I don't know what happened to Buster, he couldn't hit a target today.'"

"Have you seen Beau since Mr. Parker was arrested?"

"No I haven't, and you know that's funny. I'm surprised he hasn't been over to see about Bill. He always seemed to think so much of him. His mom and dad are divorced and Beau sort of adopted Bill as a surrogate grandfather. He and Bill have been friends for about five years now."

Jack looked at Jerry and both of them were thinking the same thing. "Mrs. Parker, do you know where Beau lives?"

"Let's see, I think he lives around the corner on Elm, the third house on the left, I believe, if I'm not mistaken."

"Jack, let's swing by and see if Beau is home. Thanks Mrs. Parker, you've been a big help."

"Beau's not in trouble is he? He seems to be such a nice young man."

Jack patted Mrs. Parker on the hand. "Right now we just want to talk to him."

When Jack and Jerry got back in the car, Jerry said, "I'm going to call the Chief and fill him in while we are driving over to Beau's house."

"Good idea."

"Chief, this is Jerry Olson. We just spoke with Mrs. Parker and there is a young man that Mr. Parker was friends with and Mr. Parker taught him how to shoot. His name is Beau Hendrix and Mrs. Parker thinks he lives over on Elm. We are on our way to speak with him now. Mrs. Parker said Mr. Parker sometimes got confused and called him Buster."

"Maybe we caught a break on this one. Follow up and keep me posted."

When they pulled up in front of the Hendrix house, they didn't see any activity. They got out of the car and walked up to the door. They couldn't see any lights on and no one responded when they rang the doorbell. "Look's like nobody is home right now, let's go grab a bite to eat and then check back later." Jack said as they walked back to the car.

Later, after they had eaten, they drove back by the house. They could see there were lights on in the living room. They rang the doorbell and this time a woman's voice called out "Who is it?"

"Detectives Olson and Oakley of the Houston Police Department."

The door opened the width of a safety chain. "Could I see your badges, please?"

Jack and Jerry took out their badges and identification and showed them to the woman. The door closed briefly and then opened to allow them entry. "Is this the Hendrix residence?" Jerry asked the woman.

"Yes, it is. What's this about?"

"Do you have a son, Beau?"

"Yes, he's not home now. Is he all right?"

"Yes ma'am. We just want to talk to him about his relationship with Mr. Parker." Jack replied.

The woman's face softened and she smiled at them. "Come in, sit down." she said and motioned them to the couch. "That old man probably saved Beau. Beau was so angry after his father and I divorced and he was acting up and running with a wild crowd and starting to experiment with drugs. Beau mows the Parkers' yard and Mr. Parker took him under his wing. I know they were lonely after they lost their son. Mr. Parker and Beau would sit on the porch and talk and drink lemonade after Beau finished mowing the yard. Beau would open up to Mr. Parker and actually talk to him. He never had much to say to me, he blamed me for the divorce. After he became friends with Mr. Parker, he stopped running with that bad crowd. Mr. Parker told him he couldn't shoot if he continued to do drugs. He would spend most of his time with Mr. Parker. Mr. Parker took him out to the shooting range and he taught Beau how to shoot. I know it sounds funny, but Mr. Parker taught him honor and discipline. I know they spent a lot of time talking about Mr. Parker's days in the army. Then Mr. Parker's Alzheimer's got worse since the first of the year and sometimes he didn't know Beau any more. Beau was devastated when Mr. Parker was arrested for those shootings. He hasn't been himself since."

"Where is Beau now?" Jack asked.

"He went on a camping trip with one of his buddies. I believe he took one of those rifles Mr. Parker gave him and said they were going to shoot some squirrels."

"Do you know where they went camping?" Jerry inquired.

"No, I'm sorry, I don't. Beau got that new black Honda truck a few months ago and he is gone nearly every weekend. He is in a lot of that survival stuff now."

"Do you know when they will be back?"

"I think they are coming back early Monday morning in time for school. He told me he would see me Monday after school."

"What's his buddy's name?"

"Hunter something, I don't know his last name. He just moved here from Colorado at the start of the school year. I don't even know where he lives. I was just glad Beau made friends with him because he needed a distraction after they arrested Mr. Parker. Hunter seems like a nice young man, very quiet and well behaved when he is over here."

"Do you know the license plate on the truck?"

"No, I'm sorry. I never paid any attention to that."

"Where do they go to school?" Jack was writing everything down.

"Memorial High School."

"Thank you, Mrs. Hendrix. If Beau calls you, please notify us. We have some questions about Mr. Parker that we would like to ask him"

They walked out to the car. "I've got a bad feeling about this." Jack said.

"Yeah, me too. I guess there's nothing we can do until Monday morning. Maybe we can catch them on their way into school."

They drove back to the station and brought the Chief up to date regarding their meeting with Mrs. Hendrix. "I'll put out a notice for everyone to keep an eye out for a black Honda truck with two teenage boys in it. I don't suppose you got a picture or a description of Beau?"

"No, we didn't want to tip his mother off that he might be a suspect in this latest shooting in case she talks to him before Monday. We'll pull a copy of his driver's license and that will get us a picture. At least, we will have an idea of what he looks like.

They went back to their desks and Jack wrote up a brief report on the meeting with Mrs. Hendrix and slipped it in the box containing files on the shootings. They finished up a few details and then walked out together. "Why don't you meet me at the station at 6:30 Monday morning and we will stake out the student parking lot and see if we can catch Beau and Hunter before they get inside." Jack said.

"Sounds like a plan to me. Be easier to talk to them before they get to class. I'll meet you here."

Chapter Twenty-Four

Jack pulled his cell phone out of his pocket as he walked to his car. Abby answered on the second ring. "Hi Jack. Did you get anything on this latest shooting?"

"We got some leads, but can't check anything out until Monday morning. Do you want to grab a pizza or something tonight? I could swing by and pick you up."

"Give me an hour to shower and change clothes and I'll be ready.

Jack decided to run by his house and shower and change clothes also. It had been a long day but he wasn't tired after hearing Abby's voice. His message light was blinking when he walked through the door so he walked over and hit the play button.

"Jack, it's mom. If you aren't working tomorrow, do you want to go to brunch with us after church? Give me a call."

Jack hit the speed dial as he was taking off his shirt. "Mom, I just got in and got your message. I'm going to take a shower and then Abby and I are going out for a bite to eat. I should be free for brunch tomorrow. 11:30?"

"11:30 should be fine. Bring Abby with you if you want. I haven't seen her in quite a while."

"Thanks. I'll see you tomorrow."

Jack showered quickly and threw on some faded jeans with a clean shirt. He slipped into some topsiders and he was ready to go. Abby came out the door as he pulled up. He couldn't help but smile as she ran down the steps. She had a white shirt tied at the waist over a red polka dotted skirt with red sandals. Her long dark hair was tied with a red ribbon.

"Mom's sleeping and dad is watching the game. I'm glad you called, I was ready to get out of the house." Abby said as she jumped in the car. She leaned over to kiss Jack's cheek, but he turned so she ended up kissing him on the mouth. He put his hand behind her head and drew her to him. Her lips were sweet and soft and he didn't think he could get enough of them. She relaxed against him and didn't try to pull away from the kiss. Surprised at her reaction, Jack kept on kissing her until they were both breathless. Slowly she pulled away from him. "Wow."

"Wow is right" Jack said. "I wasn't expecting that."

"Me either, it just sort of happened."

Jack started the car and smiled at her. "Where do you want to eat?"

"Let's go to Crabby Dave's."

Crabby Dave's was dark and quiet. The food was excellent and you could carry on a conversation without shouting at one another. The hostess showed them to a booth near the back. Abby slid in and Jack slid in beside her. He was aware of her leg pressing against his. They ordered a large sausage and mushroom pizza with fresh basil. Jack told Abby about the latest shooting but not about his conversation with Mrs. Hendrix. He didn't want to let something slip that might relate to the latest shooting. They couldn't afford to have anything come back and bite them on the butt. They lingered over their pizza until Crabby Dave's was nearly empty. Finally, Jack called for the check and they walked out. Outside, Abby slipped her hand into Jack's hand and walked closely beside him. Jack held the door open for Abby and went around and got into the driver's seat. "Where to now?"

Abby looked at him and smiled a little smile. "We could go back to your apartment."

Surprised, Jack glanced at her. "Things might get a little out of hand if we go back there."

"Jack, I'm think I'm ready to take that risk."

Jack took a deep breath and drove out of the parking lot toward his apartment. He wrapped his arm around her and held onto her, afraid she would change her mind and half-way afraid she wouldn't. They couldn't go back from this point. He parked the SUV and turned to her, "Abby…"

"Shhhh, don't say anything. Let's go inside."

Jack unlocked the door and stood aside for Abby to go by him. He locked the door and she turned into his arms. He picked her up and carried her into the bedroom. Somewhere between the door and the bed, their clothes seemed to fall from their bodies.

Hours later, she came out of his bathroom, wearing one of his shirts. The shirt was huge on her and hung nearly to her knees. Her eyes were soft and full of love for him. She came to him and wrapped her arms around him. He rested his head on the top of her head. "Abby, I love you so much. I've always loved you. Is it too soon to ask you to marry me?"

Abby leaned into Jack's embrace and her tears began to dampen his chest. "After Brandon died, I realized how unpredictable life can be. I know it's not that long since Brandon was shot, but I know I love you, Jack and yes, I'll marry you."

Jack kissed her and led her over to the couch and pulled her on his lap. They sat that way for a long time, talking softly, making plans, crying and laughing together, remembering

Brandon and crying some more. They talked about how many children they wanted and where they wanted to live and whether or not they would have a dog. Finally, Abby looked over at the clock. "Oh my gosh, I didn't realize it was so late. Mom will be worried because I didn't call. I guess I better get dressed and have you take me home."

"Tomorrow, well I guess it's today now, mom and dad want to go to brunch. Why don't you ask your folks to join us and let's tell them then. I can't keep a secret like this for long. One look at my face and my mom is going to know something is up."

"I'll ask them and I will call you in the morning, or rather later this morning."

After they were dressed, Jack drove Abby home. He walked her to the door and she stood on her tiptoes and put her lips on his. The kiss was sweet and warm and full of promise for a bright future. Jack felt the tears burning his eyes. He loved her so much it was unbelievable. He couldn't wait to tell his parents that she had agreed to marry him. He felt like the luckiest man in the world.

"Jack, mom and dad said they would meet love to do brunch. Mom is feeling so much better now, I'm glad she agreed. Where shall we meet you?"

"How about Rainbow Lodge at 11:30?"

"Man, you are doing it fancy. Great, I love you, we'll see you then."

"I love you, too. See you in a couple of hours." Jack was grinning like a fool when he hung up the phone. He immediately dialed Rainbow Lodge and requested a table for six by the windows. He told the receptionist that they were celebrating and would like to have two bottles of Veuve Cliquot Champagne chilled for them.

His mom and dad were waiting when he pulled up in front of his house. His mother took one look at him in his navy suit and red tie and raised her eyebrows at him. His dad held the door open for Karen and then he got in front with Jack. "Where are we having brunch?" His dad asked.

"I want to surprise you." Jack said.

His father rolled his eyes at Karen as Jack pulled into the Lodge's parking lot. "I hope you are paying. What are we celebrating?" he asked as he got out of the car. Before Jack could answer, Abby and her parents pulled into the parking lot and parked right beside them.

The two mothers looked at each other and grinned, already assuming why they were there. "Carol, you are looking wonderful. What a nice surprise. Jack didn't tell us you were going to join us." Karen commented.

Carol linked her arm with Karen's and winked. "Funny, Abby didn't say you would be here either."

When they got to the table and saw the champagne chilling, both mothers knew for sure what was happening. The maître d seated them and opened a bottle of champagne and poured a glass for each of them. Jack stood up and held out his hand for Abby to stand with him. "Last night, I asked Abby to marry me and she said yes." He kissed Abby and then all of them were hugging and kissing and the three women were all crying and the men were grinning like fools. Neither Carol nor Karen was surprised at the news. They had seen it coming for several weeks now.

Chapter Twenty-Five

Monday, September 17, 2007, 6:30 a.m.

Jerry came hurrying into the station. "Jack, are you ready to head out to Memorial High School?" Jack nodded and they started outside. Jerry took a close look at Jack. "What's with you? What are you looking so smug about."

"I asked Abby to marry me over the weekend and she agreed!" Jack grinned like a Cheshire cat.

"That's great. Congratulations. You couldn't let me get ahead of you, could you? Do your folks know yet?" Jerry said as he slapped Jack on the back.

"We told both sets of parents yesterday at brunch. They weren't particularly surprised."

"Well Jack to tell the truth, I'm not surprised either. Have you set a date yet?"

"I haven't even picked out a ring. I hadn't planned on asking her yet, it just sort of happened. We are going to pick out a ring next weekend. We are talking about a spring wedding."

"Maybe we will make it a double wedding." Jerry laughed and punched Jack on the arm.

They stopped at a Starbuck's and each got a large coffee and a scone then they headed out to the school. They checked out the parking lot but there were only a few cars that looked like staff cars and no trucks there yet. They backed into a spot in the student's parking lot close to the door and watched closely as the students started arriving. They had pulled the picture from Beau's driver license and were looking closely at every blond haired male student that went by. By 8:30 the lot was full and there still was no sign of the black Honda truck nor of Beau. They were about to give up when they saw it pull into the other end of the lot and park in a spot at the end of a row. Two young men in long raincoats got out of the truck. "Uh Oh!" Jack said. "Looks like they are carrying something under those coats. Let's see if we can stop them before they get to the door."

Jack and Jerry got out of Jerry's truck. "Stop, Police" Jack called out. The two boys looked over their shoulder at Jack and Jerry and took off running toward the doors, awkwardly clutching something under their coats. Jack and Jerry took off after the two young men. Jack grabbed the driver of the truck and two rifles clattered to the ground from under his raincoat. Jerry tackled the other young man and caught a rifle that he was holding. "Drop it." Jerry said. "Down on your knees now. OK, face down on the ground, hands behind you." Jack and Jerry patted the two boys down and found several pistols and boxes of ammunition."

The commotion in the parking lot caused students to gather at the windows to see what was happening. "We've got an audience." Jack said.

The vice-principal stepped outside. "What's going on out here? What are you doing to those boys?"

"Detectives Olson and Oakley, Houston Police Department. These two young men have loaded weapons and ammunition and were trying to get in the school. Please go back inside, notify your security and get everybody into classrooms and locked down. Everything is under control out here." Jack said as he took his cell phone out and called the station. We need

SHOTS

squad cars at Memorial High School in the student parking lot
on the south side of the school. We have two armed suspects in
custody." Jack hung up his cell phone. "They are on their way.
What were you boys planning on doing with those guns?"

The boys looked at each other, but didn't say a word. Hunter
started crying. "Shut up, Hunter. Don't say anything." The
driver of the truck said.

"That's ok, we will take you down to the station and talk to
you there." Jerry said and looked up as the first of two squad
cars pulled into the parking lot." After they had handcuffed the
boys, they put one boy in each squad car and the rifles, guns and
ammunition in the trunk of one of the cars. Jerry and Jack
walked up to the school and the vice principal opened the door.
"I would suggest you have your security check the students and
the building for more weapons. We don't know if those two
young men were acting alone or if someone else might be
involved." Jerry told him.

Jack and Jerry walked back to their car and drove back to the
station. "Talk about being in the right place at the right time.
Can you imagine what would have happened if we hadn't been
watching for Beau. We probably would have had another
Columbine." Jerry said referring to the school shooting in
Colorado.

When they got back to the station, they put Hunter in one
interrogation room and Beau in another. The Chief called their
parents, in Beau's case, his mother and in Hunter's case both
his mother and father. He didn't question the boys further until
the parents arrived. Beau's mother arrived first and the Chief
brought her into the room with Beau. He told her that Beau and
another boy had been apprehended at the school carrying rifles,
hand guns and boxes of ammunition and then asked her if she
wanted a lawyer present while they questioned Beau. Mrs.
Hendrix looked stricken. "Oh Beau, what have you done?"

141

Beau was sullen and unresponsive to his mother. After a while, Mrs. Hendrix decided she wanted a lawyer. Beau jumped to his feet and yelled "We don't need a lawyer. You cops think you are so smart. You arrested that poor old man and charged him with all those shootings. Mr. Parker didn't shoot anyone. I shot them all and you blamed him. You should have known he wasn't in any condition to kill all those people. You just wanted to arrest someone and solve the case. You didn't care whether he was guilty or not. All he ever did was be a friend to me and teach me how to shoot. He was a damn good teacher too. I'm nearly as good as he was now. Didn't you notice that all those people were killed with one bullet each? I shot them all from at least 100 yards away and killed them with just one bullet just like he taught me. You didn't find any casings because he taught me to pick them up. You didn't ever find my fingerprints anywhere because he taught me to wear rubber gloves when we were shooting. He showed me how to get in and out of places without being seen, where to get the best shot. How to be invisible, I walked right by you guys two or three times and you never even saw me. He taught me how to hide my weapon if I had to come back for it later. You never suspected that anyone else could have been the shooter when you arrested that poor old man. The day you arrested him, I saw those two detectives coming toward us and I told Mr. Parker to take the rifle and walk toward them as a diversion. They never even looked at me. I just jogged over to Memorial Park and ran with the other people and then went on home. Before I got my license, he used to drive me to the places, even after he got so confused. I told him I was firing blanks, that I just wanted the long range practice using the rifle with various scopes. I told him that I was pretending to be a sharpshooter just like he was. I went to Colonel Bubbie's and bought fatigues and sewed on some old insignia so he would think I was a Major. Then later on, I would give him orders as Sergeant Parker, like let me off here and pick me up at 0912 using military time. Most of the time he would revert back to his war days and he would follow orders, especially since he thought I was a Major and be right where I told him to be. He might not remember me or his own name most of the time, but he would lock onto Sergeant Parker. Part of the time he thought I was his son Johnny and part of the time he thought I was Buster somebody. Sometimes, before I got my truck, I would just take his truck without him knowing about it. He always left the keys in the ignition. I had a spare set of keys made to his gun cabinets and if he was sleeping, I would just grab a rifle and take his truck. Most of the time I could get it back without him knowing I had even taken it. "

Mrs. Hendrix looked at Beau in horror. "Beau, how could you kill all those people in cold blood?"

Beau glared at his mother. "I pretended it was dad or you when I was shooting. I would aim that rifle at their heads and say 'Goodbye mom or goodbye dad,' and then just pull the trigger. Neither one of you ever had any time for me any more. I hated everyone until Mr. Parker started teaching me to shoot. He always had time for me. He actually listened to me, which is more than I can say for you or dad. You two were so wrapped up in your own lives and your own misery and hating each other, it was like I didn't even exist. Mr. Parker told me all about his war days when he was a sharpshooter. He was the best they ever had and I am just as good. You wouldn't have caught me today if mom hadn't told you I had a rifle with me. Hunter and I were going to take out all those dumb ass people that always looked down their noses at us."

"How did Hunter get involved in all of this?" The chief asked.

"About a month ago, Hunter's parents told him that they were going to get divorced. He told me about it and man I could sympathize. That was like the worse thing that ever happened to me. I started taking Hunter out to the range and teaching him how to shoot like Mr. Parker taught me, I still had three rifles and some handguns that I had taken before the cops grabbed all the rest of them. I hid them in my bedroom under my bed. Then Hunter and me decided we would go out in a blaze of glory and shoot everyone we could and if we couldn't get away, we would shoot each other. Just like Columbine. We would be finally be somebody that everyone would remember. We would have an identity. Hunter wasn't involved in any of the other shootings. He wasn't good enough to go with me and he would have been a liability. I didn't need him anyway. Mr. Parker even gave me one of his ribbons for my sharpshooting." Beau said as he pulled the collar of his shirt down to reveal the ribbon pinned to his tee shirt. "He was so proud of me and now he doesn't even recognize me anymore." Beau broke down and started crying. Beau's mother came over and put her arm around him but he shrugged her off.

Jack and Jerry were watching the interview through the two-way glass. When Beau started crying, they just looked at each other in horror. All this death and destruction because a boy's parents never had time for him.

When the Chief finished up with Beau, he took Hunter's parents into the interrogation room where Hunter was waiting. By this time Hunter was so scared, he began babbling as soon as they walked into the room. "Mom, dad, I didn't shoot anyone. I just got caught up in Beau's scheme and by the time I got to the school, I didn't know how to get out of it. I've been so upset about you and dad getting a divorce that I just couldn't think straight."

Hunter's mom and dad put their arms around Hunter and the three of them just held each other. The Chief had them all sit down and Hunter collaborated what Beau had told them about the shootings. When the Chief had finished interrogating Hunter and returned to his office, Jack stuck his head in the door, "Chief, have you got a minute, I want to run something by you."

"Sure Jack, come on in. Great job on catching those two before they could shoot anyone at the school."

"Thanks Chief. It was just luck we happened on to Beau the way we did. I watched the interview with Beau and if it checks out, I had an idea about Mr. Parker's rifles and guns."

"I tend to believe that Beau was telling the truth and Mr. Parker didn't do any of the shootings. But we still have to check out the ballistics on the rifles we have to find out which ones were used in the shootings because they have to be kept as evidence."

"After you do that, I thought maybe we could put Mrs. Parker in touch with a reputable gun dealer to sell the guns for her. That is a valuable collection and she should get quite a bit from the sale of the guns. Combined with their social security plus what she gets out of the sale of the house and the guns, she and Mr. Parker could probably move into a nice assisted care facility with an Alzheimer's unit right here in Houston and she wouldn't have to leave her friends and her church. She is such a sweet lady and I feel sorry for her."

"That's a great idea Jack. When you get a chance, make a list of two or three gun dealers that you know are reputable and stop by Mrs. Parker's house and run the idea by her. I'll talk to the D.A. and we will try to get the rest of the guns that weren't used in the shootings back to her as soon as possible so they can be sold. One good thing is the guns are in pristine condition."

Chapter Twenty-Six

Jack was walking out to his SUV when his cell phone rang. "Jack, I am at school and one of the other teachers told me that she heard on the news they had apprehended two armed juveniles at Memorial High School this morning. Was anyone hurt?"

"No, Jerry and I just happened to be out there waiting for one of the kids in connection with the latest shooting and we saw these two young men get out of a truck. They had on long raincoats and it looked like they were hiding something under the coats. We yelled at them to stop and they started running. When we caught them, we discovered the rifles and some handguns and lots of ammunition. We disarmed them and took them to the station and one of them told us that Mr. Parker hadn't done any of the shootings. Beau Hendrix, that's his name, said that Mr. Parker had taught him how to shoot and that he had done them all. We are checking out his story but we think that is the truth. The other boy hadn't been present at any of the shootings. He just got pulled into the school deal over the weekend."

"Thank God no one was hurt at the school. Did he say why he shot all those people?"

"He was mad at his folks because they didn't pay any attention to him since they got divorced. He told his mother that he made believe that it was her or his dad as he was shooting people."

"That's horrible. Thank God you got him when you did. If that's the truth about that young man doing the shooting, what will happen to Mr. Parker now?"

Jack told her about his idea and she agreed that it was a plausible solution for Mr. and Mrs. Parker. "I'm on my way over to Mrs. Parker's now. I'll call you later. Love you!"

Mrs. Parker peeked through the curtain when Jack rang her doorbell. "What a nice surprise, come in, Jack. Would you like some coffee, I just made a pot." She said as she led him into the kitchen.

"I would love some. I think I've got some good news for you, also. We had to arrest Beau Hendrix this morning. We caught him and another young man at the high school carrying rifles and pistols. We got them before they got into the building so no one was hurt. When we got Beau to the station, he told us that Mr. Parker didn't do any of the shootings. He confessed that he had done them all. He told us that Mr. Parker had taught him how to shoot and that he had given him the rifles. I understand that Mr. Parker drove him some of the time but didn't know Beau was using live ammunition. Because of Mr. Parker's condition, I doubt that they will charge him with accessory to murder. In fact, I doubt they will charge him with anything at all."

"That's terrible news for Beau. He used to be such a nice young man. I feel so sorry for his mother, but I can't help but be relieved that Bill wasn't responsible for any of the killings. It was so hard for me to believe that he was capable of something like that. I still feel bad for all those families. What will happen now?"

"If Beau's story checks out, and I think it will, Mr. Parker could be released in your custody, especially if you have plans in place to move him to an Alzheimer's unit. I've been thinking about your situation and I may have come up with something. We, meaning the police department, could put you in touch with a reputable gun dealer who could sell Mr. Parker's gun collection for you and with your social security, the proceeds from the sale of the guns and the sale of your house, you could move into a very nice assisted care facility with an Alzheimer's unit attached. That way, you wouldn't have to leave your church and your friends and you could visit with Bill every day. Also, it would insure that Bill stays safe. How does that sound to you?"

Mrs. Parker thought about that for a moment and smiled at the suggestion. "That sounds like an ideal situation. I'm so glad you thought of it. I really didn't want to move out of Houston. Bill and I have lived here ever since he got out of the Army and I've made a lot of friends here. I'll start looking into places this afternoon."

"I'm not sure when they will be able to release Bill to your custody and they may want to know that he is going directly to an Alzheimer's facility before they do. Also, there may be a waiting list to get in some of these places and this gives you a little time to check them out. I just thought I would come by and run the idea by you to see what you thought."

"I'm so glad you did and thanks for telling me that Bill may not be the shooter. It sure helps to put my mind at rest." Mrs. Parker stood up and hugged Jack. "Thanks for coming by. Let me know about the gun dealer as soon as the guns can be released. I sure don't want them back here in the house."

Chapter Twenty-Seven

Saturday, May 3, 2008

It was another beautiful spring day. The church was decorated with white roses and yellow ribbons. The pews were packed with their friends and family. The two mothers had tears in their eyes as they heard the minister ask, "Do you Abigail take thee Jack..."